"Don't use my daughter as a smoke screen."

Nicholas Fortune's voice was suddenly harsh, his eyes flashing silver. "If it's me you're after, I prefer the direct, honest approach."

"What?" Maggie was stunned by his assumption. Inwardly she was panicking wildly. How much did he know? The unease he created in her was very pronounced at close range.

"Not that I'd ever take you up on it," he went on. "In this case, self-denial is definitely good for the soul."

"My God, you do fancy yourself, don't you?" Maggie managed to gasp out faintly.

"Oh come, Mrs. Cole, why so coy? You know damned well that there's a potent attraction between us, unwelcome as it may be. Why else have we so assiduously avoided each other?"

SUSAN NAPIER was born on Valentine's Day, so perhaps it is only fitting that she should become a romance writer. She started out as a reporter for New Zealand's largest evening newspaper before resigning to marry the paper's chief reporter. After the birth of their two children she did some free-lancing for a film production company and then settled down to write her first romance. "Now," she says, "I am in the enviable position of being able to build my career around my home and family."

Books by Susan Napier

HARLEQUIN PRESENTS

HARLEQUIN ROMANCE

Don't miss any of our special offers. Write to us at the following address for information on our newest releases.

Harlequin Reader Service
901 Fuhrmann Blvd., P.O. Box 1397, Buffalo, NY 14240
Canadian address: P.O. Box 603,
Fort Erie, Ont. L2A 5X3

SUSAN NAPIER

fortune's mistress

Harlequin Books

TORONTO • NEW YORK • LONDON
AMSTERDAM • PARIS • SYDNEY • HAMBURG
STOCKHOLM • ATHENS • TOKYO • MILAN

Harlequin Presents first edition January 1991
ISBN 0-373-11332-3

Original hardcover edition published in 1990
by Mills & Boon Limited

CHAPTER ONE

'I THINK I'm in love.'

Maggie Cole, wrapped in her morning newspaper, didn't even raise an eyebrow at her husband's announcement.

'That's nice,' she murmured distractedly, through a mouthful of wholewheat toast, wondering whether she dared look in at the advertised shoe sale between her hairdressing appointment and her lunch date with Suzy Prentice. Shoes were Maggie's biggest weakness and, even though she had never in her life needed to hunt out a bargain, the combination of SHOE and SALE in the shrieking advertisement held an irresistible allure.

'Maggie! Are you listening to me?' Finn reached across the table and snatched the newspaper out of her hand, tossing it carelessly on to the black slate floor of the dining alcove. 'I said I'm in love.'

'You said you *think* you're in love,' Maggie corrected him, glaring from her own meagre breakfast to the lavish remains of Finn's. It wasn't fair that Finn could eat like a carthorse and look like a thoroughbred whereas Maggie only had to look at a piece of chocolate to gain ten pounds.

'I think, therefore I am,' said Finn with the easy smile that bowled women over like ninepins. At six feet, with blue eyes and hair the colour of old gold and a face and physique that would challenge a Greek god's, Finian Cole could have—and probably had!—any woman he wanted. By rights he should have been a hardened rake, spoilt beyond redemption. But he wasn't, He was just... Finn.

5

A rake, yes, but a lovable one. 'I mean it, Maggie. At last I'm in love.'

'Congratulations, who is it this time? Thanks, Sam.' Maggie smiled at the lean, dark, good-looking man who scooped up the fallen newspaper and replaced it beside her plate as he refilled her coffee-cup for the third time. 'How about another piece of toast?'

'Sorry.' Sam East didn't look in the least sorry as he ignored the mournful melting of Maggie's dark brown eyes. 'Too many calories.'

'But I always have two!'

'When I know you're not going to cheat at lunch, yes.'

'What makes you think I would do that?' Maggie asked with imperious disdain.

'Because I made the reservation for you, remember? The Russian Tearoom ... blinis with sour cream and caviar?'

If Maggie could have blushed, she would have. Instead she scowled. Blinis were another weakness. 'I was only going to have one.'

'Sure you were. And I'm the Prince of Wales.'

'If you don't mind, your *Highness*,' Finn interrupted the rout, 'I'm *trying* to have a private conversation with my wife.'

'Certainly, sir.' Sam bowed himself obsequiously back into his gleaming white kitchen while Maggie giggled. Sam and Finn were the same age and, despite their different stations in life, good enough friends to insult each other with impunity.

'Maggie, will you be serious? This is *important*.'

'Sorry, darling.' Maggie composed her features, folding her hands meekly in her lap. 'You were going to tell me about the new light of your life.'

'The *only* light. This time it's real. I'm not only *in* love; I love her.'

This time there was no triumph in his voice, merely a quiet certainty that pierced Maggie's flippancy to the heart. She sobered, intently studying the seamless male beauty which she had greeted across the breakfast-table each morning for the last five years. Finn, who in looks and manner had always seemed ageless, now wore a mantle she had never seen before: true maturity. At twenty-four there were no lines around the classically cut mouth, patrician nose or smooth forehead revealed by the sinfully flattering sweep of thick blond hair. Only the cynical blue eyes revealed the extent of his considerable experience, but this morning their usual mocking dance was absent. They were deep—serene almost—and for an instant Maggie was breathless with envy.

'You're sure?' she asked slowly, although, from the look of him, the question was redundant.

His humour returned, but it was rueful rather than amused. 'Oh, yes. Very. I can't live without her, Maggie. I don't *want* to live without her. I want her to be my wife, the mother of my children.'

So. It had arrived at last; the moment of truth. Funny, but Maggie had always thought it would be her, rather than Finn, who first fell in love. So had he. After all, it was Maggie who was the romantic, the impulsive optimist. Finn was the cynic, hardened by the demands of running the retail empire built up by his grandfather and the equally strenuous demands of living up to the financial gossip columns' image as the 'Playboy Wonder'.

'Oh, Finn, I'm so glad.' Maggie leaned forward to give his hand an excited squeeze, thick, unruly, shoulder-length locks sweeping across her plate to frost inky-black ends with wholewheat crumbs. 'Who is she? Anyone I know? I didn't know you'd been seeing anyone special...you lunched with three different women last week——'

'Camouflage,' Finn grinned. 'Businesswomen all.'

Maggie sat straighter, sweeping her hair back with an impatient hand, transferring the crumbs to the dark red silk robe which flattered her Latin beauty, legacy of an Italian mother she barely remembered. 'Camouflage? Why should you need camouflage?' Her brow wrinkled under the thick, straight fringe that skimmed the fine arch of her eyebrows as she contemplated the implications. 'Finn—she's not already married, is she? Don't tell me you've fallen in love with someone else's wife?' Her disapproval was obvious.

'Would that be so shocking? After all, I'm someone else's husband—yours.'

'We're different,' Maggie dismissed impatiently. '*Is* she married?' Her heart sank at the thought of all the complications ... as if there weren't enough already. '*Do* I know her?'

'I don't think you've actually *met*.' Finn stirred a spoonful of sugar into his coffee, and Maggie's suspicions leapt to attention. Finn never took sugar in his coffee.

'Who is she, Finn?'

'You'll like her, Maggie——'

'I'm sure I will,' said Maggie, doubting it. She began sorting out in her mind all the most unsuitable candidates. She and Finn had always been utterly frank with each other. With the kind of marriage they had, frankness was essential. Finn's sudden evasiveness was very ominous. She loved him; she wasn't going to let him throw himself away on just *any*body. She sipped her own coffee and grimaced. Dared she try and sneak in a spoonful of sugar herself? She had the feeling she might need the shock-protection. As her fingers began a slow crawl to the sugar bowl, Sam dropped a pan and a string of curses in the kitchen beyond the glass brick wall and Maggie snatched her guilty hand back. She couldn't afford to put on another pound ... she wouldn't put it past Sam to have bugged her bathroom scales. He was a serious health addict and considered it his sacred duty to keep Maggie on the straight and narrow. She might attempt to outwit him on the sly but within the four walls of the apartment Sam...and guilt...reigned supreme. There was also pride involved, not to mention the spur of avoiding the genetic trap. Alongside the lean, mean Irish genes passed on by her father were the rich, voluptuous Italian plump-cells dying to turn her five-and-a-half-foot frame into an upholsterer's dream.

'So? Who is she?' Maggie took another virtuous sip of bitter black gall.

Finn muttered something, easing the salmon-pink silk tie that contrasted beautifully with his white shirt and hand-tailored grey suit.

What had he said? Laura? Laurel? Maggie's eyes widened, revealing the dark gold rim around her coffee-coloured irises. 'My God, Finn, you haven't fallen for Laura Harding, have you? She must be forty if she's a day!'

'Not Laura, *Laurie*.'

'Oh, that's a relief!' Maggie took another sip to wash the bad taste of the last out of her mouth, then sprayed it over the chrome and glass table-top as Finn cleared his throat and added,

'Laurie Fortune.'

'Laurie *Fortune*?' Maggie choked and spluttered desperately to find the breath for her outrage. 'Laurie Fortune? Is that the Laurie Fortune I *think* you mean?'

Finn nodded tersely and she recognised the slant to his jaw. He was braced to resist all objections. But still she just couldn't believe it.

'Laurie Fortune? That *child*?'

'She's not a child, Maggie. She's eighteen.'

Maggie's eyebrows disappeared up under her fringe. 'Really? She must be a slow learner. Isn't she still at school?'

A faint pink tinge showed under Finn's tanned skin and Maggie received another shock. Finn, blushing? Finn the unembarrassable?

'Finishing school,' he corrected her. 'And she left last term. She's not *quite* eighteen... but she will be in a couple of months!'

'Just what I said, a child. Finn, I don't believe this... she'll bore you in a month——'

'No.' Finn cut her off. His flush had died and that serenity she had first envied was back. 'I've known a lot of women, Maggie, but I've never known one who made me feel so... so helpless and yet so all-powerful. She's "The One", Maggie. I knew it the first time I saw her. It's nothing to do with age or experience—or lack of it. We belong together, it's as simple as that.'

'Simple?' Maggie wished it were. For Finn's sake she wished that life were that easy. 'Are you sure she feels the same way?'

Finn smiled, a tender, passionate smile that tugged at Maggie's heartstrings. Oh, Finn, please don't get hurt...

'Very sure.'

'Laurie Fortune?' Just to make sure it wasn't all some wild mistake.

'Laurie Fortune.'

Maggie took a deep breath, and plunged to the heart of the matter. 'All the millions of available women in the world, Finn, and you have to fall in love with Nicholas Fortune's baby daughter.'

Finn winced, prepared as he was for the blow. 'I told you, she's not *that* young——'

'Compared to you, she is,' said Maggie grimly. 'I presume that he doesn't know yet...?' Finn shuddered slightly, this time going pale.

'No, of course not. We've been very careful——'

'How long has it been going on?'

'A couple of months.'

'Oh, Finn.' She could appreciate the need for secrecy but, still, the deception hurt.

'I couldn't tell you, Maggie. I... it was all too new, too unreal for me at first. I couldn't quite believe my good fortune——' they both smiled humourlessly at the pun '—and ... well ... naturally we couldn't approach her father until I'd talked to you. She doesn't know, you see, about us ...'

This was a greater shock than all the others put together. Finn played strictly by the rules in all his affairs and Maggie couldn't believe that falling in love could so destroy his integrity. Contrary to his love-'em and leave-'em reputation, Finn was a very caring man. 'She doesn't know you're *married*? Finn, how *could* you!'

'Yes, of course she does.' Blue eyes flashed at the insult. 'She just doesn't know *why*. I mean, I told her that we live separate lives and she trusts me, but, well ... I couldn't tell her anything else without your permission, could I?'

Maggie caught the guilty undertone and her eyes narrowed. 'Couldn't, or wouldn't? If you really do love her, you know I would have understood your need for the complete truth between you. Or perhaps you were testing the depth of her love?' Finn looked down at his hands and Maggie knew she was right. All her sympathy was with Laurie. 'So now that you're sure of her trust you'll reward her with the truth. That was a rotten thing to do, Finn.'

He shrugged and said quietly, 'Maybe, but both she and I needed to know the extent of her faith in me. We're going to need a lot of faith to get through this. There'll be all the publicity when it comes out ... our families and her father to fight. Sometimes the only things that we'll be able to rely on will be each other's trust and love——'

'And mine,' said Maggie gently, and Finn's smile was sweet with relief.

'She *is* young, Maggie, and that did give me doubts at first. But she has the heart and guts of a woman. She doesn't want to hurt anyone but she wants to marry me. I don't deserve her, I know, after the kind of life I've lived, but I'm not noble enough to give her up. And I'm not going to, either, whatever Nick Fortune does.'

'And he can do a lot,' sighed Maggie. Biographical details about Nicholas Fortune, ruthless corporate raider, were fairly sketchy. He avoided publicity like the plague but it stalked him relentlessly, thanks to his contribution to the 'rationalisation' of the New Zealand economy by numerous takeovers of ailing companies, some of which he stripped and rebuilt, while others he merely stripped and discarded. Maggie did know that he was English, that at some time he had been a boxer and been married, that he had emigrated to New Zealand about twelve years ago, and had quickly made himself a fortune on the stock market, which he had since parlayed into several fortunes, including, both figuratively and literally, the jewel in his crown: an exclusive jewellery-manufacturing and retail business entitled simply: Fortune. The time that he didn't devote to making money he had devoted to the fiercely protective upbringing of his daughter. Laurie Fortune had only rarely been photographed and what little Maggie had heard about her suggested a sweet, biddable Daddy's girl who was being groomed for marriage to someone of impeccable social and financial standing who would continue the luxurious cosseting which had thus far cushioned her life. Not at all the sort of girl—*woman*—that Maggie had envisaged Finn falling for. She was suddenly hugely curious to see for herself.

'She'll be eighteen in a couple of months,' said Finn grimly. 'We won't need Fortune's permission for anything by then.'

'Nor his blessing? Will Laurie be happy without it? It strikes me, from what I've heard, that they're very close...'

'I know.' Finn's self-confidence fell away like a cloak. 'She says she doesn't care, that she loves me, but will it be enough?' He made a soft sound of agony. 'It *has* to be!' He got up from the table with the supple ease of his youth and vigour. 'Will you help me, Maggie?' He swung round, but it was more a demand than a request, for he knew she wouldn't refuse him his chance of happiness; they had decided on that a long time ago. 'I know we've talked about it, but a divorce at this point is going to blow everything wide open. Hell, why did I have to meet her *now*?'

'We could stick to the original plan...'

'An annulment?' Finn shook his head. 'Not unless we want the feud starting up all over again. I suppose we could——'

'Finn, why don't we leave this discussion until Laurie can join in? It's only fair—it's her future, too. When can I meet her?'

'How about tonight?'

'You have a date tonight?' Was it really that easy for them to see each other? 'I thought she went everywhere with a bodyguard or chaperone or something?'

'*Almost* everywhere,' Finn grinned, his eyes lighting with a tender reminiscence that made Maggie feel strangely hollow. Finn was her best friend. She had known, and usually liked, many of his mistresses over the five years of their marriage but she had never before felt this sense of utter exclusion.

'But actually tonight we can juggle an entirely innocent introduction,' Finn went on. 'Fortune is launching a new jewellery line this evening with a cocktail party at Sacha's' —a restaurant-nightclub they were both familiar with—'and Laurie's going to be there...'

'And her father, too, of course,' added Maggie wryly.

'Well, we can't avoid *him*. It's not as if we're total strangers. At least he can't dismiss *me* as a fortune-hunter——'

Maggie giggled, and Finn frowned at her. 'Well, there does seem to be a vast potential for puns, darling,' she placated him.

'Just don't go punning around Nick Fortune; I don't think he has much of a sense of humour.'

'Not where his daughter's concerned, anyway,' Maggie agreed.

'Dammit, Maggie, why *should* I feel bloody inferior? I have a solid family background, I'm young, at least as rich as Laurie, if not Old Nick himself, I'm healthy, I'm a respected businessman——'

'And you're married. That's the sum total, isn't it? Nick Fortune is a social reactionary. He's a puritan, Finn.'

'The hell he is. He has women——'

'But discreetly. And they're always single. He despises people like us . . . people with more money than morals, who change partners at the drop of a hat, regardless of our marriage vows . . .'

'He doesn't look like a puritan.' Finn brooded on the unfairness of it. 'Quite the opposite, in fact. In his day I'll bet he was a real hell-raiser and I doubt that morals made him his money that fast.'

'Reformed rakes make the strictest fathers,' Maggie pointed out, 'and the most jealous husbands.' She had no doubt that Finn in love would be every bit as possessive and protective of his wife as Fortune was of his daughter. 'And it still *is* his day, Finn, that's the problem. He's not forty yet, and he's faster on his feet than a lot of men half his age. He has a great deal of wealth and power, and he doesn't hesitate to use it if he's crossed——'

'Selective morality,' scorned Finn who, although an astute businessman, was a victim of his 'gentleman's' upbringing.

'Why don't you try and find things to *like* about the man?' Maggie suggested. 'After all, he is going to be your father-in-law. And you owe it to Laurie not to tear her apart with divided loyalties.'

Finn grinned. He was never depressed long. 'I like his daughter; I guess that's a start. Anyone who could produce a child like Laurie can't be all bad...'

Maggie never did get to her shoe sale. She was too busy planning strategies. Strategy was Maggie's forte. Her friends had discovered that she was a mine of imaginative ideas... as long as she didn't have to follow up with practicalities. No staying power, suggested those who envied her life of wealth and ease, but those who were privileged to know her well realised that Maggie's talent was an inventive creativity that couldn't be slotted into any particular category. It was wide and free-ranging, and unfettered by the demands of having to earn a living. Maggie was fun. Maggie could always be relied on to come up with a new idea for a party, or a fund-raiser, or a novel way around an apparently insuperable problem. Suzy Prentice, with whom she shared a distracted hour over blinis and gossip, was one of the privileged. She ran an advertising and public relations firm and was the only one who knew that the raging success of a particular new brand of pantyhose was largely due to Maggie's suggestion that this most tiresome item of feminine apparel should be shuffled on to the men who designed them. The result was a brilliant series of comic-sexy ads featuring a series of female impersonators and pompous, stuffy, business types fed up with holes and runs and bad fitting, sketched out over a series of hilarious champagne lunches. Maggie might airily confess that she 'did nothing very useful', but there were plenty to contest that!

Unfortunately this seemed to be one day when Maggie's ingenuity had deserted her. She was still mulling over ways and means to extricate herself and Finn from the tangle they had so blithely created out of their lives when they walked into the nightclub that evening. They were almost instantly photographed, the society photographer joking that he had to make the most of his opportunities. It was an oblique reference to the fact that both Finn and Maggie were frequently seen in public with other partners, but as usual they ignored the jab. Speculation about the inner workings of their weird but apparently wonderful marriage, which tranquilly endured mutual unfaithfulness, was constant, thanks to their high social profile. Theirs was a celebrity marriage that had flourished, rather than wilted, in the spotlight.

Maggie basked in it now, totally at ease, knowing she was looking her best. The hairdresser had created a new style for her that morning, different from the sophisticated sleekness she usually assumed, and she had dressed accordingly. André had permed her formerly slightly wavy hair into an effortless tangle of ebony curls, the height at the crown perfectly balancing her slightly wide mouth and jaw and drawing attention to the perfection of her olive skin and almond-shaped eyes emphasised by dull gold shadow and thick natural lashes. Her dress was fashionably short, a strapless gold and black tiger-striped satin that made the most of her regrettably generous breasts and, thanks to Sam's eternal vigilance, at the moment admirably small waist. The warm spring evening meant that she had left her legs bare and her spindly high-heeled sandals gave her the height which she felt she needed. In defiance of the occasion, the only jewellery she wore was an inexpensive lacquered-wood choker and matching slave bracelet which she had picked up on a trip to Africa. The finishing touch was the Maggie Cole trademark: gloves. She was never seen in public without them. In this instance they were wrist-length, black leather and lace, and Maggie had no doubt that the young designer who made them would soon find herself doing very good business. What Maggie wore today slavish followers of fashion would search out tomorrow...

The Fortune spring collection was scattered about the dimly lit room in illuminated glass boxes... rather hackneyed, Maggie thought, but she had to admit that the jewellery itself was anything but. Mentally she made a note of one or two of the exclusive pieces that she might like for herself, and she was contemplating a rather spectacular sunburst design in gold, platinum and yellow diamonds when Finn gave her a sharp nudge in the ribs.

'There's Laurie.'

She was over by the entrance and Maggie, who had not paid much attention to the girl the few times she had seen her before, now studied her curiously. Why, she's not even very pretty! she thought with a shock...except for her hair. It was long and loose, almost to her waist, fine and silky and a delicate shade of blonde. Her figure in a demure blue dress looked delicate, too, almost boyish in its slenderness. Goodness, thought Maggie helplessly, what on earth is Finn thinking of? He liked his women to be 'well-stacked'. One sideways look at her husband jolted her into action. She returned his nudge with interest.

'Take that fatuous look off your face, darling, you'll give the game away,' she said out of the corner of her mouth. 'You'd better start worrying how you're going to lure her away from her escort.'

The man with the possessive hand on the blue-covered elbow was Nicholas Fortune and, as Maggie looked at him, she felt the familiar sinking feeling that she always experienced when she saw the man. It was the reason that she had always given him a wide berth. On the few occasions that she had spoken with him she had made sure it was with skilfully glazed indifference, social small talk that glossed over his thinly veiled contempt for who and what she was.

He was a dramatic contrast to his daughter, not only in stature and colouring, but in manner. He was not as tall as Finn, but still tall, probably six feet, and solidly built, muscular of mind and body. His black hair was cut close to his head and liberally streaked with grey.

His face was a series of hard lines and angles, slightly
misaligned, as if the bones of his face had been broken
more than once, and, given his reputed background,
perhaps they had! That air of toughness was reinforced
by hard green eyes... or were they grey, or even hazel?
Maggie wasn't quite sure. Perhaps it depended on his
mood which, whenever she had been close to him, had
been unpredictable. In fact, the only two things about
him that contradicted that impression of repressed violence were his mouth and his eyelashes: the former surprisingly full and sensual, the latter as lush and soft as
her own. He was dressed more formally than most of
the other men present, in austere black and white, but
perhaps that was in order not to be mistaken for one of
the bouncers, thought Maggie maliciously. In everything else he could certainly pass for one. It was probably
that raw edge to him, verging on the crude, which was
attractive to women, for he certainly suffered no lack of
candidates for his rare favours.

Maggie shivered, resenting the unreasoning *frisson* of
fear that trickled down her spine. Dammit, he was only
a man, and she had handled plenty of those in her time.
Only they had all been the same kind—superficial, easily
flattered or persuaded in and out of her life, 'safe' es-
corts who were too sophisticated or too spoilt to meddle
with real emotions like love that could mess up the
comfortable life they invariably lived. Nicholas Fortune
was something else, a self-made millionaire who lived
by his own rules. Not someone who would trust without
good reason... not someone *to* trust with dangerous
knowledge about oneself. So where did that leave Maggie
and Finn? Between a rock and a hard place, both de-
fined by the man across the room.

Finn, whose whole life had so far been blessed by the
luck of the devil, appeared not to share her qualms... or
perhaps it was true that love was without fear, for a bare

half-hour later, behind a handy pillar, he introduced Maggie and Laurie.

After a few minutes of cautious, wary conversation that satisfied very little of her curiosity Maggie decided it was time for some straight talking. 'Go and get us some more champagne or something, will you, Finn?' Maggie tossed the rest of hers off and handed him her empty glass. Finn looked uncertainly at Laurie's pale features, but instead of looking unnerved at the thought of being deprived of his support she, too, handed him her glass, which was still half-full.

'Just orange juice for me, thanks.'

'Oh...uh, OK.' He was reluctant to leave, but with both women staring at him impatiently he backed off. Laurie watched him go and then cast a quick, uneasy glance around the pillar.

'It's all right, I have your father in view. He's way across the room trying to ignore some horrendous woman with a crewcut,' said Maggie, moving in for an investigative thrust. 'Doesn't your father let you drink?'

'He doesn't mind my having the occasional glass,' Laurie replied, remarkably gently, looking Maggie in the eye for the first time. 'But he doesn't dictate my tastes. I make my own decisions.'

'Good for you,' Maggie didn't pretend not to understand the challenge. 'But the decisions we make are invariably influenced by our knowledge and experience. You've led a pretty sheltered life up until now. I suppose Finn seems very glamorous and exciting from the window of your luxury ivory tower, but he's not some fantasy prince come to rescue you from boredom, he's a flesh and blood man who needs an equal partner, not a little girl just trying out her inexperienced wings.'

There was a tiny silence, and Maggie felt the stirrings of pity. Laurie Fortune's character was as insipidly innocent as her looks. Poor Finn.

'I'm sorry, Maggie,' began the girl in a small voice. 'But if you've decided that you want him after all you're out of luck. Finn asked me to marry him, and I'm not going to let him renege.'

For a moment Maggie thought she had misheard. Her eyes widened on the delicate, colourless face...it was such a contrast to those sweetly implacable words. 'You're willing to fight me for him?'

The small, pointed chin lifted. 'I am willing to fight *him* for him. Finn has this odd idea that I need protecting. I don't. I love him. He loves me. He may be married to you, but he's *mine!*'

'I'm sure other women have thought the same. He's had quite a few, you know——'

'None of them meant anything. They were just to pass the time. From now on, he has a home in me that is all he'll *ever* need.'

Such confidence! Maggie suddenly noticed the hint of steel in the baby-blue eyes. She blinked. 'I'm sorry, I'm as bad as Finn, testing you as though I had the right to make judgements. I don't. Our marriage is not and never has been a real one.' A flicker of relief behind the steely blankness. 'But I think you should know the full details before you and Finn go any further. Not——' she added quickly as Laurie opened her mouth '——because I think it'll make any difference to your loving him—believe me, you'll probably love him *more*—but because forewarned is forearmed. I'll agree he's yours, but currently he's still on loan...'

Instead of bridling, Laurie laughed, her rather prim mouth tilting up at the corners to imitate the upward tilt of her wide blue eyes. The transformation from colourless angel to mischievous gamine was revealing. She was still sweet, but with a liberal dash of pepper. All Maggie's fears melted in an instant. Oh, yes, Finn, she thought with relief, now I see...

'We'll have lunch, and a council of war,' she announced. 'Or, better still, you can come to our lawyer with us because he's the only other one who knows all the ramifications of our paper marriage. Oh, Laurie, I can't tell you how pleased and relieved I am that Finn has found someone like you. You're right, those other women were nothings. All Finn was doing was behaving like the bachelor he really is, but I was terrified that he would eventually fall for the kind of woman who gets her kicks from falling in love with married men——!' Maggie clapped her hand over her mouth when she realised what she had said, but Laurie was unoffended.

'It wasn't a kick, believe me. I was devastated when I found out that he was married... I refused to see him for weeks, but it didn't stop me loving him. That's when I knew I really loved him, when I sacrificed the happy dream of the perfect romance. I suppose I grew up. When he wrote to me... told me that yours was an arranged marriage and that you would grant him his freedom whenever he asked, that he wouldn't approach me again until the divorce was through... well...' she spread her delicate hands helplessly '...I still had doubts. My father has very strong feelings about the sanctity of marriage, and I was educated in a convent... that's a pretty potent combination.'

'Are you a Catholic? Are you worried about problems if you marry a divorced Protestant?'

Laurie shook her head. 'It was the exclusivity, not the faith, of the school which dictated its choice. In the end it boils down to whether I love Finn enough to walk through fire for him, and the answer is yes.'

'And your father?'

Laurie looked away, thinking to hide the wistfulness in her eyes. 'I don't know how long a divorce takes, but we won't be able to get married for a while. Once I'm eighteen, what can he do?' A wry grin. 'Except fire me, maybe.'

'You *work* for him?' Maggie was startled. The girl was full of surprises.

'For Fortune, the company. I'm doing a jewellery apprenticeship.'

'Really?' Maggie was impressed, but perhaps a little of her scepticism showed.

'And I intend to finish it, too. If not with Fortune, then with someone else. I've always been interested in art and design. Dad indulged me by equipping a workroom for me. I've only worked with semi-precious stones so far, but I prefer silver and gold work, anyway. These are some of mine.' She displayed the strikingly barbaric rings on four of her fingers. Now Maggie was unreservedly impressed.

'I never wear rings myself, but I know what I like. These are great! If you lose your job at Fortune Finn could always give you space at Markham's.' The prestigious mixed-retail store which Markham Cole had founded fifty years ago was the cornerstone of the diversified Cole & Co. that Finn ran, with much interference from his founding grandfather, still active though now entering his late seventies.

'Oh, I don't feel I'm good enough to sell anything yet. But I'd love to do a bracelet for you.'

'Why, thanks, I——'

'Laurie?'

Maggie had been so engrossed in the conversation that she had forgotten about keeping an eye on Nicholas Fortune. He stood beside the pillar, his eyes narrowed on the two women frozen with guilt before him. Maggie silently prayed that Finn wouldn't feel impelled to fly to their rescue. She cleared her throat, but Nick Fortune spoke first.

'Laurie? Michael Stevens is waiting to introduce you to his mother.'

Laurie stiffened imperceptibly and, mildly acquainted with the Stevenses, Maggie knew the reason. Michael was Laurie's age, a nice, very eligible *boy*. 'I ... yes, of course ... I was just on my way back from the powder-room.' Laurie pulled herself together and gave Maggie a smile of impeccable innocence. 'Nice to meet you, Mrs Cole.'

She darted away. Lucky Laurie! Maggie wasn't allowed to escape so easily. As soon as his daughter was out of earshot Nicholas Fortune spoke again, and this time the voice which had moments ago been smooth and well modulated revealed its gravelly origins.

'Stay away from my daughter, Mrs Cole. And if you don't want that handsome husband of yours to get his face broken I'd suggest you keep him on a leash!'

CHAPTER TWO

'I BEG your pardon?' Outwardly Maggie was all cool disdain while inside she was panicking wildly. How much did he know?

'You may beg all you like, Mrs Cole, but I doubt that I can put it any more simply. I want you to keep away from Laurie. She's young and impressionable, far too unsophisticated for the crowd you run with. I would like her to stay that way.'

'You can't prevent her growing up,' said Maggie haughtily, her panic easing slightly. He couldn't know, if it was Maggie he was warning off rather than Finn. 'As it happens it was a perfectly innocent conversation. I was merely admiring her jewellery....'

'From what I hear about you, Mrs Cole, nothing you do is "perfectly innocent".'

Maggie's eyes flashed jet at the cynical sneer. The infuriating thing was that in *this* case the arrogant man was right!

'And from what I hear about you, you're in no position to cast stones. You're no innocent yourself!'

'True. But I don't flaunt it the way you do. I keep my private life where it belongs. I have a responsibility to my daughter that I intend to fulfil...and that includes protecting her from herself. You're a beautiful woman, a very glamorous figure. Laurie has yet to learn how deceptive appearances can be.'

'Oh, you intend to teach her to be cynical and untrusting?' Maggie taunted, aware of the irony. Hadn't she been saying something very similar to Laurie only a few minutes earlier...about Finn?

'No, but I want her to learn that the rules that govern our society are there for a purpose. Without them, anarchy, greed and self-indulgence would ultimately destroy humankind. Self-control and self-respect go hand in hand to create a balanced, happy life. Two concepts for which, I'm sure, you never allow cupboard space.'

Mmm, she had definitely been right about reformed rakes, thought Maggie. But Nicholas Fortune was underestimating the inheritance he had already passed on to his daughter. Laurie was young but not nearly so vulnerable as he thought. She might not resemble him physically, but there was the same steely determination in her make-up. Maggie had the feeling that, given the opportunity, Laurie could be every bit as ruthless as her father in getting what she wanted. Did Finn realise it, too? Maggie hoped so, or he could be in for as much of a shock as Nicholas Fortune.

'Your daughter is almost an adult. If she hasn't learned to trust her own judgement about people, or formed her own set of personal ethics by now, then you've failed rather miserably in your responsibilities so far.'

'Come, Mrs Cole, you're the last person to be delivering a lecture on ethical standards——'

'Everyone has a right to an opinion, even fallen angels,' Maggie interrupted his gravelly drawl. She wished he wouldn't call her Mrs Cole with that cold sarcasm, as if her marital status were a bad joke. In fact, until now it had been a very good one!

'I accept that you're fallen, but I doubt you were ever an angel!' he rasped.

'Perhaps not; angels can be frightfully boring,' Maggie drawled at her languid best. He was so convinced that she was spoilt rotten, why should she disabuse him? She just wanted him back at a safe distance. The unease that he created in her was very pronounced at close range. He was all dangerous, jagged angles that could draw blood if she snagged one of them. 'So can puritans.'

Thick black and silver eyebrows rose. His eyes shifted along the spectrum from grey to blue. 'So now I'm a puritan? Make up your mind, Mrs Cole. That is—if you have one.'

Maggie was used to her butterfly intelligence being dismissed as inconsequential, so why did it offend her so intensely to hear Nicholas Fortune say it?

'Perhaps you fall somewhere in between sinner and puritan,' she said sweetly. 'Hypocrite...perhaps that's the word that my *limited* intelligence is groping for?'

'Whatever I am, it's not that,' he told her, his eyes flashing back to silver. 'I live by the code of honour I espouse to my daughter. I respect the vows and commitments that other people make, even if they don't respect them themselves.'

'And what the hell does that mean?' Maggie was angry enough to demand unwisely.

'It means if it's me you're after, don't use my daughter as a smokescreen. I prefer the direct, honest approach.'

'*What?*' Maggie was stunned by his assumption.

'Not that I'd ever take you up on it. In this case self-denial is definitely good for the soul.'

'My God, you do fancy yourself, don't you!' Maggie managed to gasp faintly.

'Oh, come, Mrs Cole, why so coy? You know damned well that there's a potent attraction between us, unwelcome as it may be. Why else have we avoided each other so assiduously?'

Maggie's eyelashes flickered with shock. She had to fight to stop her eyes from sliding nervously away from his, appalled that he had noticed something that she had, until now, refused to consciously admit. But that small sign of apprehension was noted, and Nicholas Fortune smiled. Incredibly, that hard, almost brutal face was all the more menacing for the fleeting show of humour. The smile on the face of a tiger, thought Maggie faintly...although it was she who was wearing the pelt!

She threw back her head challengingly. Unfortunately the movement thrust her satin-covered breasts into prominence, and Nicholas Fortune gave their rapid rise and fall an encompassing look of cynical admiration that further fuelled Maggie's angry dismay.

'Take your eyes off me!' she hissed before she realised how ridiculous she sounded.

'That's rather difficult, considering the goods that are on display.' But he obediently centred his narrowed gaze on her furious face again. 'You like to play games, Mrs Cole, but I don't. I'm a realist. I may enjoy a few erotic fantasies about you, as any red-blooded man would, but unlike you I'm used to controlling my appetites. If you're on the market for a new lover I suggest you direct your attention elsewhere. Your husband may not mind your promiscuity, in fact he seems to revel in it, but I find it distinctly unappealing. Even if you weren't married I doubt if I would indulge myself. I prefer a woman with old-fashioned values like honesty and faithfulness. Any attraction between us is destined to remain unfulfilled. So I tell you again: leave my daughter alone. Scraping her acquaintance will avail you nothing.'

'Difficult as it may be for you to grasp, Mr Fortune,' said Maggie acidly, rubbed raw by his casual admission of desire and contempt, 'I demand more from a man than merely crude physical attraction. You don't even *begin* to fit the bill. So you can rest your paranoid fantasies. And I'll thank you not to make snide cracks about Finn——'

The eyebrows rose again. 'A bit late to display wifely loyalty, isn't it? And sadly misplaced. Did you know that your husband is out there cruising the room, nuzzling the stray females like a stud stallion trying to decide which one to cut next out of the pack?'

Good old Finn, where better to lose yourself than a crowd? But Maggie's lack of reaction counted against her.

Nicholas Fortune's smile tautened unpleasantly. 'Of course you do. It's a feature of your "open" marriage that you both flaunt your faithlessness. Only some of those strays aren't really stray at all. I wouldn't be surprised if your pretty-boy husband was left bleeding in some dark alley one night by an outraged husband, or brother, or boyfriend...'

He didn't mention father. Thank goodness...so that opening remark about keeping Finn on a leash had only been a dig at Maggie, not a suspicion of truth. Relief made Maggie bold.

'Whatever kind of marriage ours is, it *works*, which is more than can be said for many a conventional marriage. What *really* galls you, and confounds all the vicious gossips, is that we're *happy*!'

'Are you?' His eyes darkened as they studied her, and again she felt a shiver of unease. 'Don't you feel that it lessens you as a woman not to be able to satisfy all the needs of your mate?'

It would do, certainly, if she had been in love with him. 'Not at all! Finn and I are two of a kind...we understand each other.'

'But do you understand yourselves?' he murmured. 'What is it that drives you constantly to seek new stimulation? Is it to fill some of your inner emptiness? Is it love you're looking for?' She identified a new note in the softened rasp. My God...was it...*pity*? He stepped closer and Maggie stepped back, feeling smothered. She didn't want his compassion, misplaced as it was. It made her feel soft and vulnerable, and she was neither of those things.

'Poor little rich girl,' he mocked her retreat, the compassion intensifying as he misread the reason for it. 'You've always had everything that money can buy...only now you're discovering it can't buy you love. Is that what you crave? The dream of romantic love? Do you think you'll find it wandering aimlessly from bed to bed? Don't you realise that each time you reach so greedily for it it merely slips further away? Do you wonder I don't want Laurie to board that particular merry-go-round? She has a great capacity for loving. It would be a tragedy if it was to be squandered for the sake of gaining a little surface sophistication.'

The urge to agree was almost overwhelming. His sensitivity, inside that brutally hard shell, was alarming, his paternal sincerity persuasive. Maggie's own parents had died in a Swiss avalanche when she was five but even before that she hadn't been very much aware of their presence. Her father had been a great disappointment to her grandfather. Patrick Donovan had expected his only child to take over Donovan & Co., the trading empire he had built up in direct competition with his old partner and nemesis, Markham Cole. But Michael Donovan had been more interested in spending money than making it, and so had his frivolous Italian wife. So Patrick was still at the helm of his company, though his health was rapidly failing. He had been very wrapped up in his business over the years but he had always made time for his beloved granddaughter, making sure that she lacked for nothing. But she *had* lacked. Housekeepers and governesses and companions, competent as they had been, had never quite made up for the absence of a daily family give-and-take. Maggie loved her grandfather fiercely, pig-headed and autocratic as he was, and was supremely secure in his love and affection, but no one could accuse him of being *sensitive*. Nicholas Fortune had divined more about Maggie in a few minutes than Paddy had in the last five years. It made the attraction she felt for him almost into an affinity, and the very notion terrified her.

She decided that flippancy was the only defence. 'Are you trying to appeal to my sense of decency?' she mocked in turn, and she was relieved to see that trace of compassion vanish like smoke from the grey-blue eyes.

'Do you have any?' he grated.

'What do you think?' she asked archly.

'I think...' Whatever he had been going to say, he changed his mind. His voice dipped roughly. 'I think you've been spoilt to hell and back, and it's a bloody waste.'

There was real anger in the growl, and a regret that whipped under Maggie's defences. Her eyes widened and they stared at each other for a moment; she saw the hungry male curiosity stir and the regret took on a far more personal flavour.

'Stay away from Laurie, Mrs Cole. Apart from any moral considerations, I don't think it would be wise for us to get any better acquainted than we are already...'

Maggie's mouth was suddenly dry, all the champagne she had had rushing to her head to blot out her thoughts. There were only feelings filling her awareness, uncomfortable feelings, the same hungry curiosity he had shown. It was a moment of mutual vulnerability which was shattered in a very unexpected way.

'Maggie? What's going on?' It was Finn, bristling with over-male hostility.

'Nothing.' Unfortunately it didn't come out as smoothly casual as she had intended it to. It was a very shaky feminine whisper. There was a brief flare of satisfaction in Nicholas Fortune's eyes before he dragged them away from her revealingly expressive ones and turned his hard, direct gaze on to her husband. Finn didn't turn on his charm, as Maggie half expected him to. He probably knew that charm cut no ice with this man. Instead he glared a challenge.

'Your wife and I were just...chatting.'

The pause was telling, as was the tigerish smile. To Maggie's horror she could feel her face heating up the way her body had a few moments ago. Finn took one look at her unaccustomed blush and snapped to attention.

'Well, go and find someone else to...*chat* to. Maggie and I are leaving,' he said with insolent abruptness, sliding his hand under her elbow and drawing her imperceptibly against him.

Maggie rather thought the possessive action took all three of them by surprise. What on earth was Finn playing at, coming the heavy husband?

'A pity,' Nicholas Fortune murmured. He reached for Maggie's free hand and lifted it, lowering his battered face to the black leather and brushing his parted lips over the lace-insets at her knuckles. 'Until we meet again...Maggie,' he said huskily with a well-practised familiarity that made her tingle.

'You'll have a damned long wait,' snapped Finn, pulling Maggie sharply against his side so that her hand slid out of Nick Fortune's hard, narrow palm. 'Keep away from my wife, Fortune. If you have anything to say, you can say it to me.'

The dark, menacing smile reappeared. 'You have a very beautiful wife, Cole,' he said softly. 'And a very restless one. You'd better be careful. One day someone might take it into his head to take her away from you.'

With a small, mocking bow he withdrew, leaving Finn glaring suspiciously after him.

'What the hell was that all about?'

'Nothing. He was just winding up, that's all,' said Maggie hastily. 'He caught me talking to Laurie and warned me off.'

'Arrogant swine,' muttered Finn. 'You see what Laurie has to put up with?' His attention swung back to Maggie and he frowned. 'Are you sure that's all? You two looked pretty caught up——'

'What is this, an interrogation?' demanded Maggie guiltily. 'And what was the idea of barrelling in on us like that? You deliberately antagonised him with that macho act. I would have thought that you'd try to be as conciliatory as possible——'

'I didn't like the way he was looking at you. Stay away from him, Maggie. Let me and Laurie handle him. It's our fight, I don't think you ought to get too involved.'

'Now you sound exactly like *him*,' said Maggie drily, although she couldn't imagine any two people less alike. There were few things in Finn's life he had had to fight for, whereas she had the impression that everything that Nicholas Fortune possessed he enjoyed fighting for. 'You do realise that by behaving like a typical jealous husband you've only made the situation worse? How is he going to believe that you're genuinely in love with his daughter if you're still possessive of me?'

Finn's shoulders shifted reluctantly under the fine tailoring of his cream Italian silk suit. 'Oh, hell... but, dammit, Maggie, the way he came on to you just to get at me... it just shows that he doesn't have any scruples about using people. I wouldn't like you to get hurt because of me...'

'Finn?' An unpleasant thought had just occurred to Maggie. 'It was just an act, wasn't it? I mean, you're not *really* jealous?' The last thing they needed now was for Finn to turn dog-in-the-manger.

Finn snorted, then the glimmer of his smile appeared. 'I am, actually, but of Fortune, not of you. He already has one of the women I love under his influence. I wouldn't like him to subvert you, too.'

Maggie laughed her relief. 'Don't worry, I'm a big girl now, darling, and you know I prefer my men *refined*...'

'Mmm, that's what worries me,' Finn murmured wryly. 'The refined ones have never managed to make you blush like a schoolgirl... even when you *were* a schoolgirl. All those flirtations over the years have given you a false sense of security. What happens when you finally run into a man who refuses to be taken lightly? And who takes your reputation seriously? You realise that our marriage has stolen your innocence in everyone's eyes? I owe it to you to make sure that losing the protection of my name doesn't also lose you my protection.'

'Thanks, Finn, but I might actually keep the name,' said Maggie impishly. 'You've never interfered with my life since we've been married and I'd much appreciate the same sort of treatment afterwards. Otherwise all those grubby minds are going to think you're running a *ménage à trois*. It wouldn't be fair to Laurie, or to me, though no doubt *your* reputation would be shockingly enhanced....'

Finn laughed and they dropped the subject, but Maggie was all too aware of the twin-edged sword that was her hollow marriage. She was delighted for Finn but, truth to tell, she was a little apprehensive about obtaining her freedom and re-entering the singles scene in the current liberated era, especially among her worldly contemporaries and friends. Nobody could be allowed to realise what a farce their glamorous marriage had been... not until their grandfathers rested peacefully at last...

Thomas Ritchie, their lawyer, said as much himself the next day as the three of them anxiously confronted him in his plush offices overlooking Auckland Harbour. Laurie, supposedly shopping in her lunch-break from Fortune's jewellery manufacturing premises in a converted city warehouse, was listening in awe to the convoluted story of the Cole marriage while Finn and Maggie glumly looked over the sheaf of papers that Thomas had produced from their file. Finn had sheepishly admitted that he had probably confused more than clarified when he had attempted to explain everything to her the previous evening.

'It's really quite simple,' Thomas said in the shrewd, succinct fashion that he had perfected in over a quarter of a century in his profession. He had been surprised when Finn and Maggie had approached him to act on their behalf, since it was well known that both the Coles and the Donovans dealt exclusively with, as always in their dealings, *rival* prestigious law practices. He had faced attempted bribery and threats from both Patrick Donovan and Markham Cole in their unremitting quest for information about their grandchildren, and never turned a hair. In fact, Maggie suspected he enjoyed thumbing his nose at two of the city's most powerful men...and their high-powered law firms. Thomas ran his practice with his son and son-in-law in the old-fashioned way, and Maggie also suspected that their unusual marriage provided him with an entertaining contrast to the bulk of his more mundane clients.

'Something to do with a family feud,' Laurie agreed. 'But Finn didn't tell me what started it.'

'That's because no one really knows,' said Thomas. 'Supposedly it involved Josephine, Patrick Donovan's wife, but that's only rumour. All we know for sure is that, some time after they went into partnership together, Markham Cole and Patrick had an almighty row. They sued each other over the ownership of the store that was by that time highly successful, and Finn's grandfather won. He changed the name of the store from Patrick Markham to just Markham's. Donovan went bankrupt, but a few years later he managed to open Donovan's—right down the road from Markham's—and the competition has been cut-throat ever since.

'From that day to this those two men have hated each other's guts. Their obsessive competition made them both rich men but in the end it undermined the profitability of both companies. While Finn's father was at Cole & Co. he managed to inject some common sense into Markham, but when he died of a heart attack in his early forties—brought on, so Markham claimed, by some nefarious business deal of Patrick's—the old man took the helm again with a vengeance. He trusts no one...even Finn has a hard row to hoe in trying to convince him that he knows what he's doing. As for Patrick, he has always run his company on his own... Maggie's father had no more of a head for business than Maggie does.'

Maggie pulled an unoffended face. 'The pity of it was that, instead of the dynasty they both wanted, they only managed one son each. My grandmother died in childbirth and Finn's in an influenza epidemic when his father was only five. And, because of their damned obsession with driving each other out of business, neither ever even came close to marrying again. It might have softened them up a bit if they had... and more children would have dissipated some of their infernal energy. You know, my grandfather is seventy-six and he still works a full day! In spite of the fact that he has severe breathing problems.' Maggie sighed. 'Never give up, that's his motto... even if it drives you into the grave, never give up!'

'Five years ago, it nearly did.' Thomas took up the story again. 'The grave nearly took both men, and their companies, too. Markham had started a programme of expansion that naturally Patrick shadowed step for step. It only took a rumour that one of them was interested in a company for the other one to leap in with a pre-emptive bid. Markham was having heart problems and Patrick had to carry around a portable oxygen cylinder, and maybe the intimations of mortality made defeating the enemy even more vital than ever. Because at that time all the shares were in private—family—hands, there was no accountability... both men ran their umbrella of companies like personal fiefdoms. They were literally on the verge of mutual destruction; nothing could stop them.'

'Except us,' grinned Maggie. 'Enter the conquering heroes, the sole heirs to the Cole and Donovan dynasties!'

'Except there wasn't going to be anything to be heir *to* if your grandfathers had had their way,' supplied Laurie with gamine glee. This part of the story she had understood.

'Right. I was a spoilt brat. I didn't want to be poor. I had been groomed for an inheritance all my life and I wasn't about to lose it because of Patrick's bull-headedness.' Maggie remembered the chilling blast of insecurity she had felt whistle around her carefree head after a devastating telephone conversation with her grandfather's personal assistant of seventeen years—fired because he refused to co-operate in yet another punitive takeover that would send Donovan & Co. another step towards bankruptcy. He had rung Maggie at her swank finishing school to warn her of Patrick's folly. Everyone knew that the only person able to penetrate his tough Irish hide was his beloved granddaughter. Only this time even she hadn't been able to wheedle him into pulling back, so she had turned to the only really close friend she had: Finn. He was in his last year of a degree at Oxford and Maggie had flown to England to discover that he, too, had heard gloomy rumours that the family finances were shaky.

'Neither was I,' said Finn. 'I had set my heart on taking over at Cole & Co. and I was fed up with the way that my grandfather was running it into the ground for the sake of his damned pride. We were so mad we wanted to knock their heads together!'

'But you asked Maggie to marry you instead. It's like something out of a romance,' said Laurie.

'It wasn't romantic, it was the most practical way we could think of to thwart the feud,' said Maggie. 'And actually Finn didn't ask me, I asked him!'

'She *told* me,' grinned Finn. 'She arranged for us to fly to the States and stay in Nevada for a few days to satisfy the residency requirement so that we could get married.'

'In Reno. Divorce capital of the world.' Maggie laughed at the memory. It had been like a grand adventure, a noble deed to save two stubborn old men from themselves.

'Of course, when we came back there was a furious row——'

'But I pretended to be pregnant and, with them being sickeningly old-fashioned, that shut them up for a while.'

'Long enough for Markham to discover that the devil's she-cub was actually a steel-plated darling——'

'And for Paddy to find out that the scrawny old mule's pathetic pampered wimp actually had brains and a tongue worthy of the Blarney Stone,' Maggie teased Finn. 'The first year or so was pretty rocky, especially when I had a "miscarriage" and accusations started flying around, but when they saw that Finn and I were standing firmly united they gave up the nagging. Actually I think the old buzzards are more romantic than we are, because they were quite happy to believe that we'd met and fallen instantly in love in Paris before we knew what a Romeo-Juliet cliché we were.'

'If we'd told them that we'd known each other since we were children I don't think they would have taken it so well. Madly in love they could understand, but if they'd known that we'd defied the fraternisation rule for years they might have dug their heels in,' commented Finn.

As six-year-olds they had inadvertently met one day at the park where they had been taken by their respective nannies and, aided by various sympathetic members of family staff, actually managed to sustain the secret friendship which had remained unsullied by the relentless adult hatreds that eddied above their innocent heads. Even into their teens the friendship had continued, undamaged by boy-girl conflicts. In spite of their attractiveness they had never been physically attracted to each other, which was what had made their marriage arrangements so perfect.

'But ... what will happen when you divorce?' asked Laurie, seeing the flaw in the otherwise flawless plan.

'Ah ... well ... there's the rub,' said Maggie ruefully. 'You see, originally we never thought that either of them would last very long ... their health was very precarious. We thought we could stay married for a few years and then, after the grandparents were gone, quietly get an annulment.'

'On the grounds of non-consummation,' explained Thomas. 'I have the contract here somewhere. Of course, Maggie and Finn said they only wanted a verbal agreement—they didn't want anything incriminating on record—but ... well, when you're dealing with the amounts of income that are involved it pays to have the rules laid down. The idea was to keep everything separate so that there wouldn't be any problem with matrimonial property, but the line has blurred a bit here and there. For example, they both inherited company shares when they were twenty-one—and promptly swapped them.'

'Nearly gave the grandparents apoplexy but it's paid off. They've been a great deal more cautious, knowing a certain percentage of their shareholding is in semi-enemy hands,' said Finn. 'And they've been gradually drifting towards the idea that maybe some sort of white-knight partnership might be a good thing. Both companies are attractive targets for takeover, ever since they had to make a public issue just after we were married to trade out of the corners they had painted themselves into.'

'So why did you say you were going to get a divorce?' Laurie's brow wrinkled as she looked at Finn. 'Why not get an annulment as planned? Unless ...' She stopped, her expression freezing. From looking fresh and innocent in her white dress, she suddenly looked grey and pinched.

'No, the grounds haven't been breached,' said Maggie gently. 'But if we get an annulment Markham and Paddy are going to realise that it was all a sham. We couldn't do that to their pride. It would be a betrayal of the worst kind. They're not reconciled, you know, they still go for each other's throats when they meet . . . which isn't all that often. Sometimes I get the feeling that they'd like an excuse to dig up the whole thing all over again.'

'And won't a divorce provide them with that reason?' asked Laurie dubiously.

'Not if we're very careful to make it very clear it is going to be completely amicable,' said Maggie, nibbling her lip.

'Uh-oh, she had that same look in her eye when she proposed.' Finn's blue eyes danced. 'Stand back everyone: Maggie Has An Idea.'

'No, I don't,' she admitted ruefully. 'Not yet, anyway. But I'm sure one will come. In the meantime Thomas can start discreetly processing the paperwork.'

'How long is it all going to take?' Finn got up and crossed to stand behind Laurie, with an apologetic look at Maggie. 'I don't want to rush things, but I can't expect Laurie to put up with indefinite delays.'

'Well, divorce isn't instant, you know—at least not in this country.' Thomas frowned. 'But then you weren't married here, either, so if it's instant you want you could go back to Reno.'

'The old home town,' laughed Maggie. 'Laurie could come along, too, and we could do it all in one fell swoop. Divorce and remarriage.'

The sparkle in Laurie's eyes dimmed briefly and then illuminated with her smile. 'I don't see why not.'

'I do,' inserted Finn. 'I want Laurie to have a real wedding . . . bridesmaids and orange blossom. It's what she deserves. I'm not going to marry her in some hole-and-corner mock ceremony like the one we went through last time. I'm damned proud to be marrying her.'

'It was only a joke,' Maggie told Laurie repentantly. She had learned to be flippant about her marriage but she had no right to treat Laurie's that way. A tiny ripple of envy passed through her. Would there be a man for Maggie, too, who would insist with loving tenderness on bridesmaids and orange blossom and the white gown she was entitled to?

'I know.' Laurie smiled, and the two women shared a moment of complete understanding.

Finn uttered a sigh of palpable relief, and Maggie knew that he would have been in a painful dilemma if there had been any real friction. For his own peace of mind he needed his sister-wife and the love of his life to like each other. Maggie was relieved herself that she didn't have to pretend.

The rest of the hour with Thomas was spent attending to the nitty-gritty details of separating their interests. It was agreed that Maggie should have the apartment, but there was an argument over the services of Sam East. Finn protested that she couldn't live alone with a male employee. Maggie told him sweetly that she could live with whomever the hell she liked. Laurie stepped in on the argument and suggested that perhaps they let Sam decide. Finn and Maggie accepted the compromise grudgingly, but their good humour returned when Thomas decided that as far as their shares went they should let their gifts to each other stand. Not only would it temper any action their grandfathers might take, but it would be a public indication of goodwill that would minimise the damage to the confidence of the minority shareholders if there was any open speculation about the revival of the old feud.

Maggie left Finn and Laurie conducting a fond farewell in the ramshackle lift-cage of the old legal building, while she swept off to her regular appointment at the health club in her black BMW. She didn't envy their having to hide their evident feelings for each other.

During the coming long weekend they were both attending a house-party on Waiheke Island—having discreetly bargained separate invitations from a mutual acquaintance. They would have to act like new acquaintances themselves, and be very careful not to attract any attention, but at least they would be together, even if it was in a crowd of others. Maggie, who had other plans for her weekend, hoped with all her heart that they weren't just adding to their frustrations. If Finn and Laurie never found the happiness together that they richly deserved, it would be Maggie's fault. The Grand Plan that had been concocted to thwart their grandparents' hatred had been her idea, Finn had had to be talked into it by the more reckless Maggie.

Now she needed some peace and quiet to do some more scheming and plotting. She hoped that when Finn came back from Waiheke she could present him with a new and even Grander Plan to grant him his heart's desire!

CHAPTER THREE

'It's a pity that you're not as adept at taking advice, Mrs Cole, as you are at giving it.'

Maggie, who had just finished extolling the virtues of her hairdresser to a woman sporting a sun-damaged, bleached frizz, stiffened at the low, threatening murmur. She turned slowly, giving herself time to compose her features into unrevealing smoothness.

'Oh, I take advice, Mr Fortune, but only from people I trust,' she said blandly, grateful for the protection of the oversized sunglasses she wore. Nicholas Fortune's stare was every bit as achingly brilliant as the sun.

'That must take in just about everyone here. You seem to have a very wide circle of friends.' He made it sound like a criticism. 'Is there anyone here that you *don't* know?'

'Only you,' she said sweetly. 'You seem rather like a fish out of water. You certainly don't seem to be having much fun.' What he did seem to be doing was lurking in her vicinity, watching, listening, waiting, making her wait for the confrontation she had been expecting ever since her hasty helicopter dash over the Tamaki Strait the previous night, in response to an anxious call from her husband.

'This sort of thing isn't my scene.' He shrugged dismissively, eyes sweeping disinterestedly across the lazing bodies around the huge kidney-shaped pool carved from the top of the cliff. Maggie thought it typical of their hosts' reputation for conspicuous consumption that they should build such a watery extravagance when a short

42

lift-ride down the rockface was a beautiful, clean, private white-sand beach.

'Then why come?' Why wreck Finn and Laurie's weekend?

'I didn't like the idea of Laurie coming here on her own.' The blue eyes returned to probe her dark lenses.

Maggie's dark brows arched above her frames. 'The Hunters are perfectly respectable...' A bit pretentious, perhaps, but their parties never degenerated into the kind of discreet orgies that some of the younger members of their social set favoured.

'*They* are, certainly. I have a number of business dealings with Mark. I can't, however, say the same of some of their guests.'

His attention had been caught by a passing redhead wearing the skimpiest bikini Maggie had ever seen, so the pointedness of his remark was rather lost. Maggie, herself attired in a more modest flowered bikini covered by a matching sarong and little white fingerless lace gloves, felt a pang of annoyance.

'I'm sure you'll find they have their compensations,' she snapped.

He was amused by her pettishness, quickly losing interest in the redhead as she began to flaunt herself provocatively in front of one of the bronzed young men propping up the poolside bar. Even though it was barely eleven in the morning, the alcohol was flowing freely. Maybe Nicholas Fortune was right to be worried about his daughter, except that she already had a self-appointed protector. Finn didn't spend hours at the gym to maintain his admittedly splendid physique only to waste all the effort in over-indulgence. He was the life and soul of many a party, but because of his exuberant nature, not as a result of artificial stimulation, although people might be forgiven for thinking otherwise. He was rarely without a glass in his hand at a social function, but only Maggie and the bartender knew it usually contained soda water rather than vodka or gin.

'I doubt it. You don't have to be jealous, Maggie. She may have a spectacular body, but your little cover-all is far more exciting.'

The use of her Christian name in that warm, honey-over-gravel voice reminded her of the way he had kissed her hand at the jewellery exhibition. Automatically Maggie looked around for Finn, thinking that he might be the reason for this sudden apparent intimacy, but he was nowhere to be seen. He and Laurie must be snatching some time together, hoping that she would fulfil her promise to—God forbid—distract Laurie's father. Only it was the other way around. Wondering which way to react, Maggie was startled when he leant forward and removed her sunglasses.

'I'm not jealous'—she blinked defensively—'and I happen to be wearing this because it's comfortable and I like it. I came to swim in the pool, not in a sea of male drool. May I have my sunglasses back?'

'I prefer to see the eyes of the person I'm speaking to, particularly if it's a woman.' He folded the glasses and casually slipped them into the breast-pocket of his white shirt. It was short-sleeved and revealed the mass of fine, dark hair on his thickly muscled forearms. In contrast, his biceps were smooth and virtually hairless, the same dark olive tan as his face and throat. He wore white trousers and shoes, a heavy tooled-leather black belt the only contrasting colour. Maggie had no trouble imagining a couple of holsters at each hip. That dark, rugged face, wearing its harsh lines of experience, was the perfect image of an outlaw gunslinger.

'Why?' Maggie bristled at the chauvinism of the remark. 'Do you think that a woman is less likely to lie if you can see her eyes? If you ask me, men are more shifty-eyed——'

'Who's talking about lying? I only meant that a woman generally uses her eyes more expressively than a man, to add subtle nuances to her speech,' said Nicholas with deceptive mildness. 'Your guilty tongue betrays you, rather than your eyes, Maggie. I wonder what lies you were contemplating telling me?'

Her sizzling glare was not at all subtle, and he laughed, the harsh lines of his face breaking up into attractive curves.

'Those are very expensive designer sunglasses, I don't want them lost or damaged.'

He thrust his hands into his pockets, and leaned against the low stone wall which bounded a magnificent sweeping view up the Hauraki Gulf. It was a beautiful Saturday morning with only a light breeze, and fishermen and yachtsmen were already out in force. In the distance was the hazy outline of Little Barrier Island, a bird sanctuary about a third of the size of Waiheke.

'You know, there are products without the brand name that are just as good, at less than half the price——'

'Thank you, but when I want a lecture on household budgeting I'll visit my accountant. Those were the glasses that I wanted, so I bought them. Now, may I have them back?'

'Where would you put them?' His silvered gaze slid over her cotton-Lycra sarong. 'I'll mind them for you— at least I have a pocket. You can have them back when we part.'

'You make it sound like a divorce settlement,' Maggie complained, reflexively tightening the knot just above her left breast that held the sarong in place.

'I don't believe in divorce. And settlement is just another word for extortion, in that context.'

'Do I take it that means that you're a widower?' dared Maggie. Finn had talked a lot about Laurie in the past few days, but it was all about the present, and their future together, rather than the girl's misty past. He had said, though, that Laurie didn't like talking about her mother, and that, to Maggie, bespoke trouble of some kind.

'My wife is dead, yes.'

The harsh reply made her hesitate, but only briefly. 'Your wife... or your ex-wife?'

His whole upper torso bunched. 'Mind your own damned business, Mrs Cole.'

'I'm trying to. But you don't seem to want to let me,' she told him. In her bare feet she only came up to the middle of his chest but her stubbornness gave her stature as she braved his grey-blue glare. 'You keep waylaying me with questions and insults, *Nicholas*.' She emphasised the liberty that he had earlier made of her name. 'If you can't stand the heat you know what you can do. You must have inherited your eyes from your mother... because they're very expressive—for a *man*. You don't seem to hold any fond memories of your wife. Would you still be married, if she had lived...?'

For a moment she thought, hoped, that he would swing on his heel and leave, and perhaps she let a glimmer of her triumph show for he stilled the movement even before it had begun.

'No, probably not. She was suing for divorce when she was killed, drugged to the eyeballs in a car accident. She was even more beautiful, even more spoilt than you—she had to have everything her greedy little heart wanted, *when* she wanted it. I was boxing when she married me—a rough, tough, crude thug that she could parade in front of her smart friends like a performing bear. They used to come to my fights and make bets among themselves—money, cars, drugs, sex...whatever was the fashionable coinage of the moment. And when Delia got tired of slumming, she returned to her own kind.'

Maggie was shocked, not so much by the sordid tale, but by that fact that he was telling it...to her. 'And Laurie...?'

The cynical lines in his face deepened, and Maggie felt a breathless pain. Children... they always seemed to suffer the most in adult confrontation. 'Laurie never really knew her. Delia left her, too... when she was two months old. In fact, she would never have had her in the first place if I hadn't threatened to murder her if she murdered my child. Even then, she made me pay: my child in exchange for an uncontested divorce... and virtually every penny I had.' That bleak, dangerous smile. 'She didn't need the money, she was a rich bitch—gold-plated rock. She just wanted to make me suffer for having had the gall to make her do something she didn't want to do.'

'I'm sorry.' It was woefully inadequate and, coming from another 'rich bitch', possibly even offensive but for the life of her Maggie couldn't manage anything less sincere.

'I'm not. It taught me a valuable lesson in human nature. That nothing corrupts like the inheritance of wealth and privilege. Delia was a model but she only played at it, like she played at being a wife and, very briefly, a mother. She knew she could buy her way out of any tiresome responsibilities that she might accidentally acquire. That won't happen with Laurie. I've given her the best education money can buy, but she knows that the rest is up to her. If she wants icing on her cake she has to make it herself. No cushiony trust fund to fall back on, no fond dreams of the day that they read out my will: it all goes to charity.'

'That's a bit steep, isn't it?' Maggie's eyes snapped with disapproval at his high-handed attitude. She had thought that Patrick and Markham were autocrats but this man put them in the shade! 'It looks to me as if you're punishing Laurie for her mother's mistakes——'

'The hell I am.' His clipped articulation was slipping into native harshness as he cut her off. 'I'm making sure that Laurie develops an independent sense of her identity and self-worth—and that she doesn't become the target of every two-bit hustler on the make——'

'Is that what Delia's father accused you of being?' The sudden clenching of his jaw told her that she'd hit on the truth. 'So you're making sure that history doesn't repeat itself…nobly sacrificing Laurie's inheritance while subtly reinforcing your position of male superiority. If she wants to continue to enjoy the standard of living to which you've accustomed her, she has to keep Daddy sweet——'

'That's not the way it is!' The accent was getting thicker by the minute. 'Laurie has her heart set on a career——'

'Safe in the family business, *her* business, the one you won't ever let her have. If she wants to reach the peak of a jewellery designing career she'll have to strike out on her own. Will you stake her, Daddy, if she wants to break away from your authority? If she were a *boy* things would be different!' Some of Maggie's long-ago frustration leaked through. OK, so she had no business sense, but part of her had resented the fact that Patrick had never even considered bringing *her* into Donovan & Co. She was a girl, and girls didn't bother their pretty heads with business.

'I wouldn't treat a son any differently!'

'Oh, yeah?' Maggie jeered. Such a macho man couldn't help but be a chauvinist.

'Yeah,' he jeered back, just as childishly.

There was a faint ring of steel in the air as they glared at each other. 'So why do I get the impression that you're trying to steer your independent, career-minded daughter in the direction of that hoary old chauvinistic standby— an advantageous marriage?'

His eyes narrowed. 'Who told you that?'

Did he think Laurie had? Maggie tossed her head. 'I was there, remember, when you tried to thrust Michael Stevens at her... or was it vice versa? You must be relieved that *his* father doesn't entertain your archaic puritan principles about enlightenment through hard work—Michael's inheritance runs into the millions, so I believe.'

'The Stevenses are friends, that's all. And Laurie was neglecting her duties as my hostess. You come rather hotly to her defence, Mrs Cole, for someone who barely knows my daughter. Or are you just miffed to learn that your new recruit can't afford, after all, to match the profligate lifestyle that you hoped to draw her into?'

'Oh, for goodness' sake!' Maggie was tired of that old crack and she turned aside, but he caught her upper arm. His hand was big, the knuckles slightly irregular, thick, soft hair blurring their defects.

'Who can't take the heat now?' he mocked, his accent gone. Elocution lessons, thought Maggie snidely. He might sneer at wealth but he certainly had no qualms about using it to his advantage. Unfortunately, Maggie *was* feeling the heat. It radiated from his touch to all parts of her body. Her eyes flickered involuntarily to his mouth. Oh, damn...

'Take your hand off me!' she ordered him, giving him her best 'who-the-hell-do-you-think-you-are?' look, the one that made proud men quail. Not this man, however. He smiled.

'Make me,' he told her, but there was nothing childish in the challenge. Spoken softly, it was a hard, masculine taunt overflowing with confidence. She couldn't make him do a thing and they both knew it. Or, at least, Nick did.

Maggie's eyes widened. She wasn't wearing any eye make-up but her lashes were still dramatically dark as they framed her wounded eyes. She blinked, twice, and a tiny pearl of moisture welled out of the swimming brown depths. Nicholas Fortune dropped his hand as if he'd been stung and looked at the white outline of his fingers on her tanned skin as the blood began to flow again, turning them red.

'I...Mrs Cole—Maggie—I didn't mean to...sometimes I forget my own strength...' There was dark colour under his skin.

Maggie took a swift step out of range, her tears vanishing like magic as she laughed. 'I never forget mine. I accept your humble apology, Mr Fortune. Why don't you take a dip in the pool? You look as if you could do with a bit of cooling off!'

And she ran lightly down the wide marble steps which led to the lower floor of the huge, three-storey, split-level white concrete and glass house, leaving her protagonist uttering breathy curses behind her.

As she jumped gleefully around the last curve, still full of the tingly warmth of combat, she ran into Finn and Laurie. She stared at their linked hands in horror.

'What are you doing? Your father's up there. He might be here any second.' Although, in her experience of the tender male ego, she doubted it. She had bested Nick Fortune and he wasn't going to pursue her just to watch her gloat.

'Is something wrong? You look all hot and bothered,' said Finn, reluctantly releasing Laurie's hand.

'Vamping men does that to me,' said Maggie flippantly.

'Are you talking about Dad?' Laurie looked startled and slightly horrified.

'No, of course not, we were chatting, that's all,' said Maggie hurriedly, to forestall Finn, whose eyebrows had snapped together at the idea. 'He must have seen me talking to you earlier.'

'He's suspicious, I know he is. I've never lied to him before, and now I'm doing it all the time,' Laurie's bright confidence teetered on the verge of panic. 'He had no intention of coming, you know, until the last minute. He had some business meeting or other lined up for this weekend. But then he rang the Hunters and he must have asked who else was coming. I had no time to warn Finn before I got here.'

'If he's suspicious of anyone, it's me,' Maggie soothed. 'If Elyse told him that Finn was coming he must have naturally assumed that I would be, too. But, for heaven's sake, you might try and be a bit more discreet.' Maggie's nervous alertness registered an echoing step above them and she gave Finn a hasty push that sent him backing down the stairs looking like an offended Apollo in his white tennis kit. Laurie had on white shorts and a T-shirt, too, but Maggie doubted if the flush on her face came from a hard game of tennis. Oh, to be young and in love...

'Go...go...' she hissed, waving Finn away and quickly began talking rather loudly to Laurie about her sports prowess. Two seconds later Nick Fortune appeared just above them and Maggie felt a trickle of sweat seep down her spine. He paused, grey eyes shrewdly assessing, as he said, quite pleasantly:

'Want to join me in a swim, Laurie? It looks as if both of us could do with some cooling off.'

Laurie looked puzzled at the pointed, pointless comment and Maggie rushed to her defence.

'We were just going to play a game of tennis, weren't we, Laurie?'

'What a splendid idea,' Nick drawled with deadly politeness. 'I'd love a game. Why don't you find your husband, Mrs Cole, and we'll make it a game of doubles?'

'Er...Finn doesn't play——' Maggie began wildly, at exactly the same moment as Finn made his innocent reappearance, complete with two tennis racquets tucked under his arm. Caught out in her preposterous lie,

Maggie could only stand by helplessly as the two men arranged things to their mutually hostile satisfaction.

An hour later Finn was even more hostile at having been roundly beaten, even though Laurie had done her ineffective best to temper the route by double-faulting with monotonous regularity.

'My God, you'd have thought it was Wimbledon,' he snarled, as he and Maggie made their sweaty way to the guest wing to shower and dress for lunch. 'The man set out to slaughter us. It wasn't tennis, it was war! He was going to win at all costs.' Then he added, with grudging fairness, 'Who'd have thought a guy built like a truck could move that fast? He didn't really need Laurie at all, he could have wiped the court with us without any-one's help——'

'Or hindrance. I wonder if Laurie always plays that badly?' mused Maggie. She felt as if she'd been run over by that truck. She hadn't perspired, she had *sweated*, and Nick Fortune had enjoyed seeing it. He had made her work for every meagre point she gained. He had never meant it to be a polite social game. It was an object lesson: when Nick Fortune played—anything—he played to win and to hell with the polite conventions. They had acquired quite an audience by the end of the game and Maggie was annoyed that she hadn't been able to feel her usual complacency about losing. Dammit, that was one game where winning had suddenly *mattered* . . .

'Maybe if I lost a few more games to him he might look on me in a more kindly light,' Finn went on. All his thoughts these days seemed to be headed in one direction and Maggie was beginning to feel slighted. Not that she wanted Finn herself, but it was very chastening to feel oneself in the nature of an *impediment*.

'More likely he'd despise you even more,' she snapped. 'He likes to win but he likes to win *hard*. Face it, Finn, on a tennis court you're not a worthy enough opponent.

If I hadn't been there to cover your backhand he would have won in straight sets.'

'Maybe, on the court, but off the court he won't find me so easy to handle,' said Finn pugnaciously, but Maggie could see that she had hurt him and she felt mean for adding to his undoubted suffering over Laurie. Under that handsome sophistication Finn harboured the same doubts and uncertainties of anyone in the throes of first love. Was he worthy? Did she really love him as much as he loved her? How did he look in his beloved's eyes?

'Of course he won't. Laurie loves you; that's your ace in the hole. Even if he opposes the marriage at first, he'll soon change his mind when the grandchildren start arriving!'

The idea of Nicholas Fortune as a grandfather revived her flagging spirit. It was so incongruous, the thought of that vital, virile brute as a venerated, white-haired old gentleman dandling babies on his knees. Finn's expression was disgustingly mushy as he arrived at his room. Obviously the thought of blonde, blue-eyed babies didn't ring the same humorous bells. Maggie grinned as she carried on down the black-and-white tiled hallway. Owing to the lateness, and unexpectedness, of her arrival—only Nicholas Fortune, it seemed, was naïve enough to think it natural that the Coles attended such house-parties together—she had been given a room as far away from Finn as it was possible to be. Or perhaps Elyse Hunter was merely being a good hostess, and providing sufficient leeway for any extramarital hanky-panky that her guests might wish to privately indulge in.

Maggie's secret humour was dimmed at lunch, when she discovered that some imp of mischief had placed her directly opposite Nick Fortune. The table was wide and the floral centrepieces lavish but she was still within striking distance. Worse, she was sandwiched in between two indolent young men whom she had dated on and off over the years and who cheerfully expressed their rivalry for her favours. Ordinarily Maggie would have enjoyed their harmless flirting, but today she felt that every smile condemned her. However, smile and flirt she did, anything to keep Nick Fortune from noticing his daughter further down the table, exchanging small intimate glances with an unusually subdued Finn.

The fat was shovelled further on to the fire when a chance remark by another guest expressed surprise at seeing Maggie at all. Nick was quick to pick it up.

'Do you mean that you didn't intend coming? What changed your mind?'

You did, she wanted to snap, remembering the lovely spa bath she had been enjoying when Finn had rung, pleading for her camouflaging presence on the island. Maggie had been sure that some of his distraught helplessness had been charmingly exaggerated for effect, but there was no denying that they needed her and she *had* said that she would do all she could.

Instead she batted her eyelashes and covered the truth with an outrageous costume. 'Why, you did, Nicky, darling,' she drawled, to the laughter of her companions. 'I heard that you were coming and I just *couldn't* stay away.'

Instead of looking uncomfortable or annoyed at her breathlessly coy admission, Nick Fortune smiled thinly.

'Snap, Maggie, *darling*.' He bettered her husky drawl.

'Uh-oh, I think we've got some competition,' joked the idiot on her left, when Maggie seemed lost for words.

'Maggie's democratic, I'm sure there's enough to go around,' responded the moron on her right.

'More than enough, judging by the number of kilojoules you're putting away,' Nick mocked, his challenging eyes falling to her plate.

Maggie dropped her fork and followed his gaze, appalled at what she saw. Without thinking about it, she had helped herself to the most fattening dishes from the buffet. She stared at the remains with horror. 'Oh, no, Sam is going to kill me!'

'Who's Sam?' Nick asked, intrigued by the note of fear in her voice.

'My conscience,' she groaned. 'I'm going to be on bread and water for a week if he finds out. Except...' one daintily-gloved hand fluttered in relief '... I *did* just play a strenuous game of tennis, didn't I? All this probably just makes me all square.'

'Square you're not!' declared the moron, with a gentle leer at the figure-hugging bodice of her crisp spring dress.

'Who's Sam?' asked Nick again, and the idiot answered him.

'Haven't you heard about the famous Cole *ménage à trois*? Lucky Sam lives with Maggie and Finn.'

'Sam is our housekeeper,' said Maggie quellingly.

'And more besides!' The idiot had brought his sister with him, who had always envied and attempted to undermine Maggie's classy image. She leant forward now, to confide maliciously to Nick, 'Maggie once said that Sam was the glue to her marriage. And he's such a hunk—sexy Sam, she calls him! You're so lucky, Maggie, to have *two* gorgeous men at your beck and call. I don't know how you keep them both from fighting over you, but then you've always been good at juggling *men*.' The significance of the plural escaped no one and all within earshot looked expectantly at Maggie. She could always be relied on for a flip answer. No one expected Maggie to take anything seriously, insults included.

She didn't disappoint them. 'I was trained from a very early age,' she told Nick gravely. 'When I was five my grandfather bought a toy manufacturing company and I used to market-test their range. I had dozens and dozens of male dolls, far more than female ones because the company made mainly boys' action toys. Since then I've sort of naturally assumed that males are more fun by the dozen.'

Nick didn't even crack a smile. 'I see. You mean you graduated from boys' toys to toy boys?'

The table broke up, but for a moment Maggie didn't smile either, then her wide mouth began to quiver at the corners with the effort of matching Nick's blandness. He had no such trouble. He watched and waited, until she could outface him no longer and gave in to the overwhelming pressure of her laughter. Her helpless mirth destroyed her sophistication, a mauve glove, one shade darker than her dress, came up to cover her giggles as her brown eyes danced with approval of his pun, even though it was against her.

Only then did he allow himself to reflect the jousting good humour around him. But his smile was for Maggie alone, an intimate acknowledgement of victory, as if he had known that she didn't want to think of him as witty or amusing, capable of holding his own against her determined flippancy. She had wanted him to feel awkward, out of place, even socially inept in his self-confessed puritanism—it would have given her more confidence in her ability to deceive him. Instead he had neatly turned the tables, deflecting back on to herself her subtle attempts to discomfit him. There was no question that he didn't belong in this atmosphere of determined frivolity, but it wasn't because he didn't fit in, it was because he didn't even try. He was here for his daughter's sake, and for her he would put up with the boredom, the inane chatter. What *did* he like to do in his spare time? Maggie wondered. Or was he like her grandfather, who never seemed to have any? What about the women who satisfied his puritan requirements—when did he fit them in? Sandwiched between business appointments? Did he have a convenient couch in his office?

Maggie realised she was still staring at him, and flushed at her thoughts. Instantly the blue-grey eyes darkened to sea-green... what was *he* thinking about? She didn't want to know. She pushed the plate of fattening goodies firmly away from her, a Freudian rejection that wasn't lost on the man across the table. Maggie tore her eyes away. Oh, no, she might be spoilt—used to getting everything she wanted—but she wasn't stupid! Nick Fortune was out of bounds for a number of reasons, all of them excellent.

Determinedly she threw herself into the general conversation, ruthlessly ignoring Nick Fortune's unnerving, unwavering attention. What was he trying to do, for goodness' sake? Make her feel like a gauche, self-conscious teenager? Maggie had never been gauche in her life, she had been *born* possessing all the social charms, and she didn't intend to start now! Dammit, why didn't he turn his battered sex appeal on that blonde floozy beside him, whose flirting was utterly failing in its objective? *She* was available—Maggie, as he had so coolly told her, wasn't.

After lunch Maggie felt in need of a nap and then, while the afternoon sun was still blazing, she took the lift down to the deserted beach and stretched herself out on the silky-warm sand with a current bestseller. The water was still too spring-chill for a swim—the pool above was heated to blood temperature for the sybarites—but Maggie dabbled her feet at the edge every now and then, enjoying the refreshing salty bite around her ankles.

Overhead the sounds of merrymaking drifted on the breeze but Maggie resisted its lure. She *wasn't* hiding, she told herself, just enjoying a little well-earned peace! It was inevitable that, sooner or later, Finn should have come looking for her and dragged her off to do guard duty, although luckily by this time the floozy seemed to be making some headway, and Finn and Laurie and Maggie were able to drift around the luxurious grounds of the 'weekend cottage' largely unobserved by parental authority. Laurie talked easily about her life, and the more she heard the more Maggie liked her. This wasn't a young girl rebelling against her strictly controlled life by experimenting with intrigue. She didn't expect life with Finn to be a bed of roses without the thorns. If anything, she was less starry-eyed about it all than he was!

At dinner Maggie was relieved to find that the seating had been shuffled and she was well away from both Laurie and Nick. The woman beside her was a tireless charity worker who had more than once come to Maggie for fresh ideas for her galas, and they fell into an animated conversation about the hassles of stimulating the jaded captains of industry into digging deeper for worthy causes. Maggie remembered some of her ideas that had horribly misfired and the conversational ripples widened as some of their immediate neighbours recalled Maggie-inspired triumphs and disasters. Either way, one of them pointed out, Maggie's participation always garnered plenty of publicity, for when one of her brainwaves failed it always did so with magnificent style! Dinner took care of the rest of the evening, for someone wanted her advice about an upcoming fair and Maggie was in her element closeted in the conservatory with coffee and liqueurs and handmade chocolates, kicking around crazy ideas with practised flair. When she flagged she was surprised to see that it was after midnight, and she took herself off to bed with yawning satisfaction, shrugging off the effusive, slightly inebriated gratitude of the lady who now had a perfumed notepad full of possibilities.

Maggie had showered and changed into the beautifully flowing blue silk nightgown that could have passed as a balldress when she felt a pang of remorse. Had Finn and Laurie managed to sneak any time together, while she was enjoying herself? Impulsively she tossed on her matching *peignoir* and let herself out into the dim hallway. There was no answer to her gentle knock on Finn's door, and when she ducked her head inside the room was empty. It didn't really surprise her—no doubt

there were some who wouldn't make it to bed at all tonight—but Maggie decided to wait for a while. She had
to talk to Finn, persuade him to leave, as he should have
done the minute he knew that Laurie's father was ac-
companying her. They would achieve nothing this
weekend but to reinforce Nick Fortune's image of Finn
and Maggie as morally bankrupt. Her initial impulse,
to choreograph a fight scene to lay the ground for the
break-up of their 'perfect modern marriage', had died
in that first clash with Nick. Public dirty-linen washing
would not impress him at all. Maggie frowned, remembering that he hadn't given her back her sunglasses. She
wouldn't ask for them, she'd rather do without. She
didn't want to ask Nick Fortune for anything...ever...

When she woke and looked at her watch again it was
4 a.m. and she was still alone. She sat up, working the
crick out of her neck. Damn you, Finn, where are you?
If she found out he had gone to Laurie's room she would
wring his gorgeous neck! *Both* their necks...! Surely
they wouldn't be so foolish as to take the risk of being
discovered in such compromising circumstances? Surely
even love wasn't *that* blind to the scandalous
consequences?

Oh, well, waiting around worrying about it wouldn't
help. She might as well go back and spend what little
remained of the night in her own bed. Let Finn and
Laurie do their own worrying. The tiles of the hallway
were cold under the soles of her bare feet and she shivered
as she skipped around a curve, and ran slapbang into
the arms of someone coming the other way. Powerful
fingers bit into the slippery drapings over her slender
arms as their bodies briefly danced for balance. Maggie
didn't even need to tilt her head back to see who it was;
she knew from the first, shuddering contact.

'Don't tell me—you can't sleep and you're on your
way to the kitchen for a glass of hot milk,' Nick Fortune

murmured in a low, sardonic voice as he set her away from him and surveyed her silken beauty, the ruffled black mane and sensuously soft brown eyes, still big with sleep.

'Of course I'm not,' she hissed, rejecting the thinly veiled sneer. He wouldn't have believed it, even if it had been true. 'For your information I'm on my way *back* to my room——'

Stupid! The sardonic brackets around his mouth deepened. 'From the bathroom, no doubt...' He offered another insulting cliché, knowing full well that each sumptuous guest-room had *en suite* facilities.

Maggie flushed angrily. If only he were similarly undressed she might be able to fling some of his dirt back at him, but unfortunately he still wore his darkly flattering dinner-suit—dining here was always a formal affair—although the black tie was unfastened, along with the first few pearl buttons of his white shirt. 'From my husband's room, actually.'

His sceptical expression was infuriating. 'You have to sneak around to be with your own husband?'

'I am not sneaking around,' she told him furiously, endeavouring to keep her voice down in the high-ceilinged, echoing hall. 'We were given separate rooms——'

'I understand that's par for the course in your very flexible marriage. So...you've just spent almost an entire night with your husband. It must be something of a record for you both...'

There was something guarded in his eyes that made Maggie hesitate before she blasted him. Was she just being ultra-sensitive or was he goading her? What did he know that she didn't? Had he seen Finn himself...somewhere else? 'I've been in his room, yes,' she said carefully, hoping he wouldn't notice the evasion. Vain hope!

'Wasn't he there, Maggie? Is that why you're restlessly prowling the halls?' The guarded expression revealed nothing, but his rough voice was gentle, and he lifted his hand to brush his knuckles against the proud angle of her chin.

Maggie wanted to knock his hand away, but just in time she remembered what the long lace ruffles at her cuffs hid and she didn't think she could take any more of that velvety compassion right now, so she suffered his touch in haughty silence.

'Why do you let him do it to you? Are you a masochist? Do you *seek* humiliation? Is that why you came here, because you suspected your husband was embarking on another affair? Did you hope your presence might prick his conscience? Does he even have one?'

'You...you don't know what you're talking about,' Maggie said weakly, sinking deeper and deeper into the mire. It was obvious that Nick's contempt for Finn was far greater than his contempt for Maggie. But how to redress the balance?

'I know there must be something badly wrong for a beautiful woman like you to sacrifice your pride.' His hand had moved to her throat to find the pulse that beat so wildly there. He stroked it with his thumb, and Maggie's eyes closed and she shivered helplessly. 'What's wrong, Maggie...? You can tell me...'

For a moment, there in the hushed quiet of the dim hallway, under the magic spell of his hypnotic touch, she almost did. Then she remembered: this is the enemy. She flinched, dislodging the fragile link. His fingers dropped caressingly away and she opened her eyes. The dark hunger in his, restrained as it was, shocked and frightened her. She felt his anger pressing against her mind. Was he angry because she hadn't fallen easy victim to his ruthless gentleness? Or because he resented wanting her?

'Nothing's wrong.' She fiercely denied her moment's weakness. He made a sharp movement with his massive shoulders and there was a glint against the dark fabric. A wavy blonde hair clung to his lapel. Maggie sucked in a breath. Was *that* where he'd been until four in the morning? And he had the *gall* to make insulting assumptions about *her*!

Maggie plucked the hair from his jacket with her right hand and held it up disdainfully. 'Pick this up in the *bathroom*, did you?'

'The lady and I were dancing,' he said evenly. 'She retired hours ago.'

'To touch up her roots, no doubt,' Maggie snorted scathingly, flicking the offending evidence away. 'But then perhaps you prefer bottled blondes to the real thing!'

She swept past him, but she didn't get the last word.

'Bitch,' he said softly, almost admiringly, and Maggie's knees were weak when she shut her door on his disturbing presence. How did he manage to make an insult sound like a compliment? He had been laughing at her, she knew he had, and she couldn't blame him. She had sounded for all the world like an aggrieved wife!

CHAPTER FOUR

MAGGIE was breathless as she climbed off the Jet-Ski and handed it over to the eager-looking young man impatiently waiting on the jetty. He took off in a shower of spray, heading towards the other five Jet-Skis, criss-crossing the waters of the bay. As Maggie leapt down the jetty steps to the beach she tossed a grin at Elyse Hunter, whose ample figure was lolling royally on a sunlounger.

'Your neighbours must hate you,' said Maggie, gesturing towards the irritatingly high-pitched buzz of the Jet-Skis. 'All this and a helicopter, too.'

Elyse shrugged plump, freckled shoulders. 'As long as they can hitch an occasional ride, they put up with it. And one of them has a powerboat that makes a hell of a lot more noise than we do.'

Maggie walked over to where she'd left her towel, draped over one of the chairs that had been transported down the cliff so that no guest had to worry about intrusive grains of sand ruining a coiffure or a costume...or a drink. The black and yellow nylon-Lycra gloves, designed to match her sleek *maillot*, slipped on the zip of her wetsuit and she struggled to pull it down. The Hunters had a variety of full and half wetsuits available for the guests, but the only one left when Maggie had decided to take a turn on the Jet-Ski had been slightly too small. It had been a devil to get into and seemed to Maggie to have shrunk. She made a sound of impatience and began to strip off her right glove with her teeth when a shadow blocked out the sun.

'Here, let me...'

'It's all right, I can do it.' Maggie's protest was muffled by her glove as she scrabbled for the cord attached to the tab. She yanked but nothing happened. She wrestled fruitlessly for a few more moments, getting more and more desperate, until with a grunt of male exasperation Nicholas Fortune brushed her hands out of the way.

'I said I can do it,' she said abruptly, trying not to flinch when his fingers slid inside the close-fitting neck of her wetsuit to support the zip as he sought to release it.

'I know you did,' he murmured, concentrating on his task. His eyes were lowered, narrowed on the trouble-some tab, and Maggie reluctantly admired those long, fine lashes . . . as thick and silky-looking as the hair on his arms and broad, impressive chest. There were a number of very handsome men on the beach this morning but Nick seemed to overshadow them all. His body might not have the tanned and sculpted symmetry of some of the younger men, but there was an animal vitality in his compact toughness that was uncompromisingly male. He wore a pair of modest navy boxer swimming trunks but somehow managed to look more nearly naked than a number of those flaunting themselves in sexy briefs. Maggie had noticed the sidelong feminine glances that he had been ignoring all morning and knew she wasn't alone in her approval, but she would have died before she admitted it! She tried to twist away.

'Look, don't bother, why don't I just——'

His fingers, hooked into the suit, held her easily. 'Don't be so damned impatient.' The muscles of his chest and shoulders bunched against her feeble resistance and Maggie subsided limply, telling herself she was getting hot because of the extra insulation, not because of the proximity of that overpowering masculinity.

'Ah . . .' With a soft growl of satisfaction Nick found and disposed of the small obstruction. He began to ease the zip down slowly, careful to avoid further snags. The sensation of release from the tight, clammy constriction was exquisite, and Maggie sighed luxuriously. Nick hesitated, and she suddenly became conscious of the intimacy of the situation. He peeled the zip another couple of inches and Maggie quickly put her hand below his, on her waist.

'Thanks, I can do the rest now.'

Nick toyed with the cord briefly before releasing it, as if considering ignoring her husky command, but if she had thought the aura of intimacy would vanish when she tackled the job herself, she was mistaken. Nick stood and watched the progress of the tab all the way to its final resting place. Then he stood there, making no attempt to hide his interest, as she struggled to peel her arms out of the top half of the suit. Her *maillot* was modestly cut but extremely sleek and by the time she had wrenched her legs out of the tenacious wetsuit she was flushed with angry awareness that Nick's sea-dark eyes had studied every inch of her. He seemed particularly fascinated by the movement of her breasts and she knew why. She bent and picked up her yellow-striped beach shirt and slipped it on, casually arranging the buttonless lapels over the betraying hardness of her nipples. When she turned he was still there, and he had the nerve to be smiling slightly, eyebrows raised, mocking her attempt to hide from the shared knowledge that her body had enjoyed his slow survey.

'Pity,' he said, and she didn't ask him to explain, haunted by a vivid image of his hands moving down her body, parting her wetsuit to find her naked beneath. Thrusting the fantasy sternly away, Maggie sat down on her lounging chair and concentrated on replacing her glove.

'To even *swim* in those things. Isn't that carrying vanity too far?' said Nick, inviting himself to sit down on the unoccupied chair next to her.

'Gloves are my trademark. I wear them everywhere,' said Maggie, arranging her hat so that a shadow fell across her eyes. He still hadn't returned her sunglasses. She was quite content for everyone to believe that her gloves were purely an affectation.

'Everywhere?' The gravelly voice was amused, speculative... 'Even to bed?'

Maggie gave him a disdainful look that told him it would be a cold day in hell before *he* ever found out. Actually, she had wondered herself... Only a few people outside her family had seen the extensive scars on her left hand and, apart from the doctors, those who did usually recoiled in pity or distaste. When she did finally find a man whom she could love, should she show him the scars before...or after...? He might prefer not to feel the callused ridges of the scars sliding over his skin, catching in the dark hairs—— Oh, no! Maggie wrenched her gaze away from the slow rise and fall of that muscular chest.

'I suppose your mother taught you that a lady never risks soiling her fair, unblemished hands among the unwashed masses. Perhaps it's less a trademark than an obsession.'

Unblemished. If only he knew! Maggie laughed, surprising him. 'I suppose it *is* kind of an obsession, but only in the fashion sense. In fact, it's very bad etiquette to wear gloves with a swimsuit, and *really* rotten form to eat and drink in them, but these days who cares as long as you make an impact? As for my mother, I understand that ladylike was the last way to describe her. She enjoyed life to the hilt. She died the way she lived— when I was five—my father, too.'

'You understand? Don't you remember anything about her?'

Maggie shrugged at what was common knowledge. 'My parents were great travellers—if I didn't have photographs of them I probably wouldn't even know what they looked like. Mother was Italian and she preferred the European climate and lifestyle. A baby definitely didn't fit into their jetsetting schedule, so I was left here with my grandfather.'

'Do you resent that?' Out of the corner of her eye she could see Nick stretching, flexing those brutally tough muscles, but she kept a resolute eye on the sea.

'Not really. Paddy—my grandfather—was pretty wrapped up in his business, but he never treated me as if I was a nuisance. He was always there when I needed him.' Her mouth curved in a reminiscent grin. 'In fact, I had a whale of a childhood. I pretty well ran wild, driving countless nannies crazy, until——' Absently she rubbed her left hand. Nick's eyes narrowed, but his curiosity was destined to remain unsatisfied. Maggie pulled herself from her reverie and tossed her head in her characteristic gesture of carelessness. 'Until one day Paddy decided that indulgence should be tempered by discipline, and when Paddy makes up his mind there's no stopping him! I hated school at first, after having been able to wind governesses around my little finger, but I adjusted. I enjoyed the company of my peers, having spent most of my time until then around adults. Those poor teachers, they managed to get me to *act* like a lady, even if they couldn't get me to *think* like one. I'm living proof that genetics triumphs over environment. I'm more like my mother than Paddy. I enjoy my life too much to spoil it with pointless regrets or brooding about the past. I certainly won't let my past shape my future.'

'Does that mean that there's no room in *your* life for children?' Nick adroitly sidestepped that pointed challenge.

'Not at this point. But it's an experience that I wouldn't like to miss.'

Nick's mouth twisted. 'Is that all motherhood means to you? Another *experience*?'

'In the sense that if I didn't have children I'd feel that I hadn't explored my full potential as a woman, yes,' said Maggie coolly, refusing to back down under the implied sneer. 'On the other hand, I won't be pushed into having a baby because it's *expected* of me. That kind of commitment shouldn't be entered into lightly, and certainly not when——'

'When the marriage of the prospective parents is shaky?' he suggested, when she bit off the rest of her sentence. 'From bitter experience I would have to agree.'

Maggie would have liked to blaze out in righteous indignation, but if she defended her marriage it would just make things harder for Finn. Instead she said tartly, 'A good proportion of the population would have never been born on that criterion. Would you rather that Laurie had never existed?'

'Of course not.' His eyes swivelled out to sea and narrowed against the glare as he watched his daughter on one of the distant Jet-Skis. 'Sometimes our greatest mistakes can become our greatest achievements.'

'Is that what you consider Laurie? *Your* achievement?' Maggie bristled on the girl's behalf.

'My God, but you're touchy today,' he murmured. 'Did you get out of the wrong side of the bed this morning? Or perhaps—given your absence at breakfast—it was the *right* side of the *wrong* bed...'

Maggie choked before she found her voice, furtively checking to make sure that they weren't being overheard. 'How dare you? I thought we established last night that——'

'That you're more vulnerable than you generally let on. And a woman who feels betrayed the way you were is liable to seek to ease the pain in the easy pleasure of revenge.'

'If you think that I'd sleep with someone just to get back at Finn——'

'Not necessarily that, but to reassure yourself, perhaps, that you're still a desirable woman.'

'I know exactly what I am,' Maggie gritted. 'I don't need you or any other man to tell me. And I wasn't feeling betrayed, that was just the product of your lurid imagination——'

'It wasn't a product of my imagination that I saw your husband disappearing down here to the beach with someone, just before I came along to bed,' Nick said quietly and Maggie blanched at how close Finn had come to discovery...the irresponsible fool! No wonder Nick had doubted that she had been ensconced in marital bliss last night! Maggie glared at the Jet-Ski riders, singling out her husband. With a jolt she noticed that the rider next to him was Laurie.

'I'm sorry, Maggie,' he said, more softly still as he misjudged the reason for her shock, 'but it can't be that much of a surprise. It was what you expected, wasn't it? What is it that makes this time different from the others?'

'What are you—a tycoon or a marriage guidance counsellor? Your qualifications aren't very impressive, you know; you couldn't even make a success of your own marriage, so don't start casting stones at mine!'

The tip of her lash drew blood but he didn't flinch, his voice taut with control as he said evenly, 'That's just what qualifies me to express an opinion. I'm intimately familiar with the destructive games that married people can play, and the pain it can cause the innocent.' His eyes darkened as they dipped to her veiled curves. 'I wouldn't exactly call you an innocent, but you aren't as cool as you make out. I think you *do* resent your parents for excluding you from their magic circle. I think you've tried to armour yourself against caring too much, and that's why you selected a lightweight for a husband, one who wouldn't demand too much from you. Only now you find that it's not enough and you're starting to wonder whether Cole will ever be able to fill the empty places inside you. You're tense, nervous and there's a rather desperate quality about you . . . as if you're on the brink of doing something reckless . . . anything . . . to free yourself from the mink-lined trap that you created for yourself.'

There was a little, swooping silence. Maggie was appalled at his perspicacity. How could they hope to fool a man with such shrewd insight into human nature? Thankfully, his conclusions were way off-base but, dear God, how well he read her!

'Finn isn't a lightweight!' she forced herself to say coldly. 'If he plays hard it's because he works hard. Just because he makes his success *seem* effortless doesn't mean it's been easy to achieve. It hasn't, especially with his grandfather second-guessing every decision. So don't you sneer at Finn just because he had advantages that you didn't. That's reverse snobbery and it's just as bad as the other kind. Finn and I don't judge people by the circumstances of their birth!' Her temper had risen with every word she uttered, sabotaging her cool hauteur.

'How broad-minded of you,' he murmured sardonically, needling her, watching her wonder where and how to throw the next punch. Nick hadn't spent years in the brutal sport of professional boxing without learning the defensive importance of working one's opponent to assess his weaknesses. Maggie Cole had handed him hers on a plate: her early lack of self-discipline had left its lasting mark. When her strong emotional impulses were triggered she tended to speak and act first and only stop to think about the consequences when it was too late.

To a seasoned fighter like Nick she should have been an open book, but there were too many inconsistencies for him to entirely trust to instinct. The mild suspicion which had persuaded him to come to the island with his

daughter had deepened into a nagging certainty. There
was something between Laurie and Maggie Cole that he
was missing, some connection he had yet to figure out.
If the lovely iron butterfly across the table from him had
been a smoker he had no doubt that she'd have been
puffing away like a chimney by now. He made her
nervous—quite apart from the acknowledged attraction
that quivered between them—in fact, she was looking
more strung out with each passing moment. What in the
hell was going on? Drugs? Was she high? Her great dark
eyes, which seemed fixed on something over his left
shoulder, looked oddly dilated. If she had a drug problem
that would explain the somewhat bizarre swings of mood
she seemed to be experiencing. Nick's mouth unconsciously straightened into a grim line. If Maggie Cole
was trying to introduce his daughter to a drug habit she
had every right to be nervous. All the wealth and influ-
ential friends in the world wouldn't be able to save her
from his avenging rage. Nick felt charged with ruthless
energy, the familiar race of adrenalin that he usually felt
before a fight pumping through his veins. Before this
weekend was over he'd know Maggie Cole like the back
of his hand. And he'd put a stop to whatever it was she
was up to.

'You were very young when you eloped with Cole,
weren't you? If you were as beautiful and headstrong
then as you are now I would guess that the opposition
from both families was a spur rather than a
discouragement...'

It didn't surprise Maggie that he had heard the gossip
about her marriage. What did surprise her was the heady
feeling that his backhanded compliment gave her.
Beautiful and headstrong... It was an improvement on
spoilt and promiscuous!

'If you're implying I was too young to realise what I
was doing you're wrong. Whatever happens, I'll never
regret marrying Finn,' she said, but she wasn't concen-

trating on her words. She hadn't even noticed Nick's face harden with his suspicions; she had been too busy agonising over the fact that both Laurie and Finn had ridden in to the jetty and were now sauntering back down the beach, the essence of casualness. If Maggie stayed where she was the four of them would be expected to socialise, and she didn't think she could stand it. She jumped to her feet, babbling something about having had too much sun.

Laurie tried to stop her leaving, probably for the same reason that Maggie wanted to go, but her father just lay back in his chair, regarding Maggie's agitation as she hustled Finn away with an air of sardonic triumph that she longed to douse with a bucket of water!

The weekend did not improve. In fact, as far as Maggie was concerned it limped from disaster to disaster. Nick Fortune, that shadowy, restrained figure on the fringes of boredom—the kind of semi-reclusive guest that was the bane of every hostess—was suddenly Mr Personality. His former aloofness had resulted in the other party-goers closing ranks on him, but once he had proved he could be as hedonistic as the rest of them he was welcomed with open-armed relief: no one wanted to be on the wrong side of Nicholas Fortune.

Except Maggie Cole. She watched with furious distrust as he ingratiated himself effortlessly into the tight inner circle protectively formed by leaders of Auckland's social set, charming them all with his brutally cynical wit. He showed all the tact and skill of a dedicated social-climber, but Maggie knew that he didn't give a damn about his social standing. So what was he after? Information? She shuddered to think what privileged gossip he might now have access to. Once you made the inner circle you were trusted with secrets that the common herd were denied—while the rest of society might speculate about who was doing what with whom and why and how, the privileged few, thanks to their myriad sources of information, usually knew enough of the facts to sort them from the fiction. She and Finn had been very careful to maintain their particular fiction even among their best friends, but that hadn't stopped the occasional dark rumour.

Maggie was stretched to the limit, monitoring all Nick's conversations and movements, while at the same time trying to keep track of Laurie and Finn, juggling vainly to keep them all away from each other. Unfortunately she received no co-operation in her valiant efforts. Nick evidently wasn't letting his daughter out of his sight and Finn had no intention of relinquishing his covert claim to her company. It wouldn't have been so bad if either man had maintained a mannerly pretence, but under cover of the general conversation they continued to exchange bland, biting comments that barely masked the mutual hostility. Dammit, couldn't Finn see that he was being goaded? In her attempt to defuse the tensions in their persistent little group Maggie was reduced to flirting madly with the nearest available male, but even that managed to backfire on her.

'What in the hell are you doing leading Charles on like that?' Finn hissed in her ear at one point. 'The guy already fancies himself half in love with you. Or do you *want* him to make a nuisance of himself?'

Knowing the strain he was under, Maggie almost forgave him—particularly since she hadn't even noticed the identity of the man that she was exchanging flip innuendoes with. Charles was a nice boy, but very immature. 'What I'm doing is trying to distract people from noticing what an idiot you're making of yourself!' she whispered back furiously. 'Sooner or later they're going to wonder why you're suddenly so touchy...and put two and two together. Why can't you back off?'

Finn snapped a short laugh. 'I will if he will.'

'Oh, for goodness' sake, you sound about eight years old. And you're acting it, too. Can't you see that you're making Laurie miserable!'

That was her ace. A scowl marred Finn's handsome features as he turned away and Maggie's breath caught in her throat when she saw who had come up behind him.

'Marital spat?' enquired Nick with all the bold innocence of a poacher caught holding a loaded elephant gun.

'Why don't you go and pester someone else with your crass attentions, Mr Fortune? I'm beginning to find them very tiresome,' she said haughtily, figuring that she had nothing to lose by being offensive.

'Is that what I'm doing?' he murmured. 'And here I thought that I was fitting in so well with your gushing group. It seems to me that I'm the only man in it *not* pestering you. No wonder your husband is getting tense. Are you deliberately trying to make him jealous?'

So he hadn't overheard what they were saying. All Maggie could come up with in her relief was a ragged 'Oh, shut up!' She hooked on to a passing male elbow, and found herself sliding out of the frying-pan into the flames in Charles Stevenson's eyes as he quickly manoeuvred her into the privacy of a small shaded arbour and there proceeded to deliver an impassioned declaration of his undying devotion. Normally Maggie would have given him a gentle set-down that would have salvaged his pride and their friendship, but she was just about at the end of her tether, fed up with the entire male sex. Instead she told him not to be a fool, which immediately made it imperative for him to prove otherwise. Charles was a husky young man, whose ardent embraces weren't easy to fend off, and when she began to get really angry he responded with righteous indignation.

'Damn you, Maggie, there's no one around, you don't have to pretend. You weren't worrying about your husband before. No one has to know... You want this, you know you do...!'

So much for undying devotion. It was the story of her life, these hurried propositions in dark corners, although Charles hadn't even bothered to wait for dark...sunset was at least an hour away! And she was supposed to be persuaded because he dressed up his lust in a few threadbare romantic frills...

'No, Charles...you misunderstood. *Charles!*' Maggie twisted and turned her head to try to avoid his eager mouth. The way he was holding her she was afraid she'd crack a rib.

'Misunderstood, hell!' he growled, too aroused to acknowledge her struggles, intent on making the most of his opportunity. 'You've been throwing me those come-hither smiles and hints all afternoon——'

'For God's sake, Charles, that was just party talk!' Maggie wished she'd paid more attention to Sam's attempts to teach her a few tricks of self-defence.

'You mean, it was all just a tease?' Charles' voice was thick with frustration. 'Why am I an exception? You don't say no to other men.'

In other words, why couldn't he have a piece of the action, too? 'Have you ever thought that maybe those other men were lying?' she demanded acidly. 'Maybe I'm not as indiscriminate as their pride makes out.'

'They can't all be liars——'

'Why not? *You're* going to lie, aren't you?' Maggie accused bitterly. 'Whether I say yes or no, if anyone asks you how far you got with me you're just going to smirk and let your silence lie for you.'

She thought she had him for a moment, but when she tried to ease away he jerked her back. She debated screaming and then decided against it. Charles had had a few drinks but he wasn't going to rape her right here

and now, he was just going to maul her about a bit to
salve his ego. She kicked him, to remind him of her objections, and he swore and hurt her with his mouth.

Suddenly she was free, Charles dangling by his sleeve
from Nick Fortune's powerful fist.

'She was asking for it——' the angry young man was
blustering in the face of Nick's grim distaste.

'That's what they all say,' said Nick drily, but to
Maggie's chagrin she heard a note of sympathy in his
voice that evidently also registered with Charles. He immediately lost some of his defensive aggression, as well
as his fear, as Nick continued softly, 'However, in this
case you may be right. Still, a gentleman always accepts
a refusal, no matter how belated. If he doesn't he can
find himself in all sorts of strife.'

Charles took a step back as Nick released him and
dusted off the crumpled sleeve of his designer shirt. The
gesture, though friendly, held an unmistakable threat.
'Take my advice, old boy, steer clear of married women,
they're more trouble than they're worth. And, Charles'—
pleasantly, as he began to hurry away—'gentlemen don't
kiss and tell, either...'

'What would you know about being a gentleman?'
said Maggie tartly, as Charles beat his hasty retreat and
the cold grey gaze was turned on her somewhat shaky
self.

'More than you know about being a lady, evidently.
Aren't you going to thank me?'

'I could have handled him without your interference!'

'Could you? You hadn't handled him very well so far.
Or perhaps that was deliberate. Do you like it rough,
Maggie?'

'I don't like *it* at all.'

'So you are just a tease?'

'You can talk, you...you peeping Tom!' Maggie could
feel herself flushing with humiliation at what he had seen.

'First you eavesdrop, then you snoop around looking for dirt——'

'Fortunately I found it. Calm down, Maggie. Nothing happened.'

That hint of male conspiracy again. 'You call being assaulted *nothing*? Oh, yes, I forgot, you used to do that as a career, didn't you? Well, what's nothing to you is a great deal to me, Mr Golden Gloves!'

His eyebrows rose. 'You want to lay charges? I'll be happy to be a witness.'

'I bet you would! For the defence or the prosecution, I wonder.'

'You mean there's some doubt?'

She glared at him, cornered. 'I was only flirting. It didn't oblige me to sleep with him, dammit! It's a party, for goodness' sake, everyone flirts at parties.'

'So you said.' He looked at her as she smoothed back her hair with hands that barely trembled. 'Are you often assaulted by men you've led up the primrose path, Mrs Cole?'

'Of course not. Most men aren't uncivilised apes!'

'Charles struck me as being a very civilised young man. Far more so than I am, for example...'

Maggie blinked. His eyes had gone from grey to blue. Had he moved closer? She licked lips that still stung slightly.

'I really don't think this conversation is going anywhere, do you?' she said, in a weak and belated attempt at diplomacy. 'I didn't mean to snap at you, I was upset, that's all. Of course it was kind of you to help me...' She dazzled him with a flattering smile.

'Very prettily said.' Nick was unimpressed. 'A pity you don't mean a damned word of it.'

What was he, a mind-reader? Maggie's smile dimmed a fraction and she pouted, which impressed him even less.

'Stop it, Maggie.'

'Stop what?'

'Flirting with me. Don't you ever learn by your mistakes?'

Her smile vanished altogether. 'I'd have to be mad to flirt with a pious bastard like you.'

'Crazy,' he agreed. 'Foul-mouthed, too. I don't like women who swear.'

'You don't seem to like women who do *anything*,' she snapped, flicking her eyes over his aggressive masculinity.

'You're flirting again.' He raked her over with his gravelly drawl as her mouth opened to repudiate his warning. 'Although I suppose it's second nature to you— you probably don't even realise you're doing it . . . which makes it all the more dangerous. One day you're going to run into a man who won't be wound around your pretty little finger, who'll take you seriously and who'll want more than a few stolen kisses to satisfy him. Next time there might not be anyone around to pull him off you. In future, Mrs Cole, I'd advise you to put up or shut up. In these days of increasing female assertiveness there's a lot of male rage and frustration lurking around. Unless you're actively seeking to be dominated I'd ease up on the tease. Stop trading on your sex—— '

'What do you want me to do—become a nun?'

'I don't think you have the vocation.' A touch of humour ghosted across his face. 'But maybe you need one. Maybe boredom is at the root of all your problems.'

'I certainly feel a yawn coming on. If you lecture your daughter this way no wonder she——'

'She what?'

'She's such a dutiful daughter,' Maggie ad-libbed quickly, cursing her unwary tongue. 'But the time will come when you'll have to let her make her own mistakes.'

'As long as they're her own, and not just an imitation of other people's. For someone so incredibly self-centred you show an awful lot of interest in Laurie. Ludicrous as it might seem, one might almost accuse you of being *protective*...'

Exposed once more by his shrewdness, Maggie fell back automatically on her womanly wiles, forgetting that he had already seen through them.

'Oh, dear... found out. And here I was thinking I'd impress you with what a marvellous stepmama I'd make.' She covered her coy smile with a gloved hand, a little-girl gesture that usually made men laugh.

Instead of being amused, or acidly pointing out that she was married already, Nick stared at her. She could see his mind ticking over behind those narrowed blue eyes. That shrewd mind worked in a way so totally alien to hers that it was impossible to track his thoughts, but his long silence increased her nervousness.

'Nick.' She stopped, marshalling her scattered thoughts.

'Maggie?'

Whatever she had been going to say went totally out of her head at the way he said her name, as if wrapping it in roughened velvet.

She tried again. 'Nick...' He was going to be angry, when he found out, but he was going to be hurt, too, and suddenly she couldn't bear the thought of it.

'Maggie,' he repeated, and it was almost a sigh of resignation. He reached out and brushed away a blossom which had drifted down from the arch overhead and landed on her bare shoulder. The creamy flower slid down her smooth golden skin and caught in the elastic neckline of her off-the-shoulder gypsy blouse. Her first impulse was to pluck it out herself but she couldn't make her hands move. After a long, tense moment Nick's shadow fell across her and his finger dipped beneath the elastic to scoop out the errant flower. It was a brief courtesy but it wasn't casual. Maggie closed her eyes as she felt his knuckle scrape across her skin, leaving a tingling warmth in the soft valley between her breasts.

'Maggie.' This time her name was a breath beating against his resistance. She opened her eyes. 'It's too late, Maggie. Years too late, for both of us. You stay on your side of the fence, and I'll stay on mine...' But he was looking at her wide, crushed-rose mouth and she swayed instinctively towards him.

When their mouths touched there was an explosion of heat, a sweet eruption that quaked through Maggie and left her weak and shaking. No other man had kissed her, touched her... only Nick. His mouth was bold and intoxicating, like rich red wine that lingered on the palate. His tongue moved in her mouth, tasting the tart sweetness of her surrender, curling around her tongue and enticing it into an uninhibited exploration of its own, drawing her skilfully into his possession so that he might suckle her with a slow, erotic rhythm that shocked her un- tutored senses. He didn't touch her with anything but his mouth, and Maggie didn't dare unfold her fists clenched at her side for fear that if she touched him she would never let him go... But for the pleasure he gave her they might have been naked on a bed, locked in each other's arms.

When the kiss broke, something in Maggie did, too. Her eyes were wide and dark with a new and frightening knowledge. Nick sucked in a breath, pale beneath his tan, his mouth lush and full, a counterbalance to the shocking hardness of the rest of him.

'No.' He answered her unspoken question, self- contempt stiffening his spine. 'Consider this hello and goodbye, Maggie. It's not going to happen again. I want no part in another broken marriage.'

'You can't break what doesn't exist,' Maggie said wildly, stricken by the feeling that she had lost some vital part of herself—forever.

His hesitation was too brief to register. He pivoted on his heel. 'Goodbye, Maggie——' He came to a dead stop. Through the lattice-work of the arbour he caught sight of another couple exchanging a laughing kiss of casual intimacy, so different from the torrid embrace Nick and Maggie had just shared, but no less betraying. He made a raw sound in his throat and Maggie felt the world collapse around her ears.

'No, Nick——' She caught at him as his muscles bunched for action, as if he would have physically torn his way through the shrubs and landscaped barriers that separated him from his daughter.

He swung on Maggie, his eyes boiling with black rage, stripped of any lingering softness. 'Why? If I kill him you'll be well rid of him, you can play the merry widow to your heart's content!'

There was no sign of the cynical tycoon; this was a man who lived by his fists, primitive, elemental in his brute rage.

'Nick, you can't just rush over there and make a scene.' With difficulty she clung to his shirtsleeve. 'What would that achieve?'

'A great deal of personal satisfaction. My God, I said he'd end up bleeding in a dark alley——' He shook her off, but she managed to dart in front of him, stumbling as she tried to slow him down.

'Nick, for God's sake, stop for a moment and think!' To her shock he did. The big hands flexed slowly, and he jerked his head sharply, as if throwing off the effects of a solid punch.

'You knew,' he realised. 'You knew your husband was interested in my Laurie. My God, you knew.' It was too much to hope that he wouldn't make the next connection, his voice thick with loathing...and the north-country accent that was usually buried under suavely-coached vowels. 'You knew and you were running interference. Weren't you? *Weren't you?*'

Maggie had dreamt of being held by him, but not like this, dangling between those bruising fists, being shaken like a rag doll.

Nick, please——'

'Weren't you?'

'I—— Yes. Yes. *Yes!*' He threw her from him and she nearly fell.

'And I thought it might be drugs. I thought it was drugs when you were really pimping for your husband.' He laughed at his naïveté.

'Now, hold on a minute——'

'Get out of my way, Maggie, or I'll go through you——'

'Sure you will. Brute force always wins through.' Maggie was desperate. 'But you'll scare the hell out of Laurie if you go wading in throwing punches. Isn't it illegal for professional fighters to hit people? That'll make a terrific impression on your daughter, won't it? Beating an innocent man to a pulp and getting arrested!'

'*Innocent——?*'

'All right, not so innocent,' Maggie cut him off. If she could talk fast enough she might be able to temper his rage. 'Instead of going off half-cocked——'

'I would say that was Cole's speciality, wouldn't you?' Nick snarled, still straining at the metaphorical leash, but at least he wasn't smashing forward now. He was merely killing with his glare. Thank God Finn and Laurie had stopped fooling around and were just sitting on a stone bench, talking.

'Nick, your daughter is a mature young lady, she's not going to do anything stupid, especially with you here. Nor is Finn, for that matter. The only person contemplating doing anything stupid right now is you. If you're worried, talk to Laurie. But listen, too, don't just start firing commands.'

'What makes you such an expert on my daughter?'

'The same thing that makes you such an expert on rocky marriages. My grandfather just loved to issue orders—in fact he still does. If he hadn't been so determined to force me into his mould maybe I wouldn't have

felt pushed into eloping with Finn.' It was a justifiable
lie, she told herself, because it very well *might* have happened, if financial circumstances hadn't pre-empted
everything else. Maggie knew several women who deeply
regretted the rash marriages they had made to escape
unbearably restrictive home lives.

It worked. Nick cooled a few degrees—from red-hot
rage to cold bloody murder. 'You suggest that I pretend
not to have noticed?' he demanded savagely. 'Sit back
and watch my daughter get hurt by an arrogant swine
who obviously doesn't give a damn for anyone else but
himself? The hell I will! You tell your husband to look
elsewhere for his thrills, Maggie, or I'll break him into
little pieces and scatter them into the fires of hell.'

His menacing sincerity sent a shiver of fear down
Maggie's spine. Nick's threat was almost gloating, as if
he would *enjoy* the chance to expend his rage in violence. Finn wouldn't stand a chance.

Nick saw her expression, and his smile was as lethal
as his rage. 'Oh, don't fret, Maggie, I won't lay a glove
on him. But he'll wish I had! What I'll do to him will
feel far worse than a mere physical beating. Tell him,
Maggie. If you love him at all make him believe you,
because if you don't and he seduces my daughter I'll gut
him of everything he has, slowly, so he can see and feel
his life shrivelling away from him, bit by bit. So either
warn him, or stand clear. I don't want to hurt you but
I will, if I go after Cole, and once I start nothing, and
nobody, can stop me!'

CHAPTER FIVE

MAGGIE cautiously peered round the door at the empty foyer of the apartment. Grinning to herself, she stepped in, quietly shutting the door behind her, and, taking care to keep the metal-tipped heels of her Valentinos well up off the slate floor, began to tiptoe across towards the curving staircase and the sanctuary of her second-floor bedroom.

'Been shopping, madam?'

She squeaked and spun around, smiling weakly at Sam as she hurriedly thrust her clutch of shopping bags behind her back.

'Just a few things I needed.'

Sam's eyebrows rose knowingly. 'You and Imelda Marcos both.'

Maggie frowned. 'I'm not that bad, at least I don't *hoard*.' Shoes were made for *wearing* and showing off, not for gathering dust in her dressing-room. When she tired of a pair, or no longer wore them more than three times a month, she bundled them up and regretfully sent them off to the local Salvation Army shop.

'Shoes for every day of the *month*, that's what you said. I counted fifty-two last time I vacuumed in there,' said Sam smugly.

'But I wear more than one pair a day,' Maggie pointed out. 'Sometimes I wear three or four. So I *could* have a hundred and twenty pairs in there and still keep my promise.'

'In letter, maybe, but not in spirit,' said Sam. 'I hope you kept the receipts.'

84

'A couple of measly pairs of shoes. Sam, don't be a nag!'

'What did they do, give you a bag for each shoe?' he asked drily, having done a quick count of the ill-concealed bags.

'Very funny, Sam.' Maggie's eyes narrowed maliciously. 'I think I feel like chilli tonight. Hot and spicy. Maybe I'll invite a few friends over, so make it a *big* pot.'

Sam had once confided that an unfortunate culinary experience in South America had turned him off chilli peppers for life. Even the smell of them cooking made him feel nauseous. He blanched slightly at the very suggestion, but recovered nicely. 'You've got company already.' He jerked his head towards the closed door of the library.

'Why didn't you say so?' Maggie cried, glad of the diversion. She hadn't *meant* to buy any more shoes, but since she was passing the store she had just popped in to browse and...well, one thing led to another. 'Be a darling and put these away for me.' She pushed the bags in his direction, rubbing it in. 'Who is it?'

'Your grandfather.'

Maggie frowned. 'I wonder what he wants? We're supposed to be having lunch together tomorrow...maybe he can't make it after all.' Not waiting for an answer to her speculation she clicked across the hall, freezing as Sam added, with a tinge of friendly malice himself, 'And Markham...'

Maggie's jaw dropped as she cranked her head around to stare. 'They came *together*?'

'No. Your grandfather's been here for half an hour. Markham arrived about ten minutes ago.'

'And you put them in the same room?' Maggie's voice rose in horror. 'They've probably killed each other by now!'

Sam shrugged. 'Markham barged in without a by your leave. And I haven't heard any gunshots.'

Maggie rushed over to the door and listened. Ominously, she couldn't hear a sound. She beckoned to Sam and he hoisted the bags.

'Excuse me. I have to put these away. Then I have to bring out my gas mask.'

'Sam!' Maggie hissed, furious with him as he turned on his heel and calmly left her to deal with whatever was beyond the hushed door. 'Sam, I was only kidding about the chilli,' she wailed to empty air.

Taking a deep breath, she opened the door a crack and peeped through. Immediately the door was wrenched out of her hand and Markham Cole stood there, a slim, dapper man with a thick head of impossibly brown hair and a carefully cultivated moustache that was currently twitching angrily.

'What're you doing, skulking around out there, girl? Eavesdropping? Typical Donovan manoeuvre!'

'Hello, Markham.' Maggie gave him a kiss on a surprisingly smooth cheek, knowing the insult hadn't really been aimed at her, but at the man glowering on the other side of the room. 'What a surprise. I didn't expect to see you today.'

Her grandfather barked a laugh. 'Of course you didn't. Markham always was full of surprises. None of them pleasant. Always popping up where he's least wanted, shoving his nose into other people's business, sniffing around like a sewer rat for the corpse of someone else's deal.'

'I wasn't expecting you, either, Paddy,' said Maggie, calmly going over and giving him a kiss, too, which he scrubbed off sourly. Short and stocky and nearly bald, her grandfather looked like the rough, tough Irishman he was. 'Er...would you like a drink?'

'I helped meself.' Paddy prodded the empty whiskey glass on the marble-topped desk with the head of the stick which he had needed to use ever since his illness at the time of Maggie's marriage.

'Don't you always,' sniped Markham spitefully, giving the lie to that dapper self-confidence. 'No wonder you don't have any friends left, old man, you've stolen them blind for years.'

Patrick Donovan bristled. 'Some friends ain't worth having anyway...and that you're handy with the Grecian 2000 and buy yourself a new face every few years doesn't make you any younger than me. But then you were never much for showing your *real* face to the world, were you, Markham, old boy? You always did hide behind that mask of so-called respectability——'

'Have another, why don't you, Paddy?' Maggie dashed into the fray, pouring a healthy slug of best Irish into his glass and hurriedly thrusting one at Markham before he simmered over.

A heavy silence reigned as the two men drank, watching each other, so intent on the animosity between them that they ignored Maggie's nervous chatter about inconsequentials. The brooding went on for some time until Maggie realised that neither man wanted to come to the point of his visit first.

'Oh, for goodness' sake!' she burst out at last, having knocked back a couple of whiskeys herself, trying to figure out how to be diplomatic. Normally she hated the taste of strong liquor, but the explosions going on in her belly did seem to bolster her courage. 'If neither of you has anything to say I don't know why you bothered to come...certainly not to see me. Why don't I just leave and you two can sort out whatever's bugging you?'

It was like firing a blank from a starter's gun. The two men were off and running, throwing punches at each other every step of the way. Maggie listened to the welter of accusations and counter-accusations with growing horror. Someone, under cover of a series of nominee companies, was buying up Cole & Co. *and* Donovan shares, soaking up the extras on the market and luring several long-term holders to surrender their blocks. So far the total percentage was still low, but creeping high enough to attract attention, and to start a few rumours. Markham was convinced that Patrick was buying Cole shares to weight the hinted-at merger in his favour while Patrick believed that Markham was trying to sabotage it altogether and substitute a hostile takeover. When she managed to sift out the fact that the mystery buyer had entered the market the previous week Maggie's heart sank.

Nicholas Fortune! It had to be him; the timing was too fortuitous for it to be just a coincidence. With what she'd thought was supreme restraint Laurie and Finn had agreed between themselves not to meet for at least a week after that benighted weekend, to give Laurie's father time to cool down. They hadn't stopped communicating, however, spending hours on the phone to each other every day, and for Nick Fortune that was obviously a clear signal of intent. Now nothing, and nobody, could stop him!

'Now look, you two!' Maggie yelled over the top of the two old men going hammer and tongs. 'Finn and I are fed up with the way you carry on. In fact, all this hostility is putting a strain on our marriage. A *great* strain.'

That got their attention. Open-mouthed, they both stared at her.

'A *very* great strain,' Maggie added for good measure. If Nick Fortune was acting on his threat everything would have to be speeded up even more . . . as though it wasn't breakneck enough already! 'In fact . . . we're thinking about a separation . . .'

'Separation?' Markham suddenly seemed to sprout grey hairs before her eyes.

Patrick was purple, verging on the apoplectic. 'Over my dead body!' he roared. 'No *Donovan* ever runs out on a marriage.'

'Now, Paddy——'

'Don't you Paddy me! I never wanted you to marry that grandson of a two-faced snake in the grass in the first place, but you did and that's that! I never did like the loose way you run your marriage but that's your business. You ain't a little girl any more to come crying home when things don't go your way——'

'If you two had had a few babies by now you wouldn't be blithely talking about separating. I hope you don't have any of those crazy feminist notions of *finding* yourself——'Markham put his oar in and promptly had it chopped off.

'Ain't necessarily Maggie who's crazy, Markham Cole. Maybe that smart-assed boy of yours ain't got any babies to give——'

'He got her pregnant in the first place, didn't he?' Markham reacted strongly to the slight on the family masculinity, and they were off and running again. Maggie was about to burst into tears with frustration when Sam appeared dramatically in the doorway.

'You're popular tonight, Maggie. Someone else here to see you.'

Anything to break up the fight. Maggie rolled her eyes. 'Roll 'em in, Sam.'

'You sure?'

He looked a little too virtuous for Maggie's liking, but she was in no state to ponder it. 'Oh, for goodness' sake, Sam, don't be coy. I don't care if it's the Pope.' The two old men were actually buffeting each other with their chests, and she planted a firm hand on each to hold them apart, thereby missing Sam's grin.

'Yes, *ma'am*!' He backed away obsequiously. 'Come right in, Mr Fortune.'

Markham and Patrick stopped flailing and Maggie, sandwiched uncomfortably between them regarded the newcomer in wide-eyed panic.

'A new parlour game?' Nick Fortune enquired smoothly.

'No, an old one. It's called Family Feud,' murmured Sam behind him and Maggie shot him a vitriolic look.

'Thank you, Samuel, you may go.' The words were acid etching in ice.

'Yes, your ladyship.' He winked at her. 'Good luck, honeychile.'

Maggie could feel herself flushing as Nicholas Fortune followed the byplay. Lord knows what he was thinking as his eyes narrowed at Sam's casual familiarity, flickering over the handsome face with well-concealed distaste.

'Well, well, well...' Patrick dissociated himself from the mêlée and thrust out a welcoming hand. 'Nick Fortune. Don't believe we've met in more than passing. Heard a lot about you, though. You're a friend of Finn's? Never mentioned it to me, Maggie.' He directed a needle-sharp stare at his granddaughter.

'Mr Fortune is more an acquaintance than a friend, Paddy,' she said quellingly, glaring daggers at the man coolly shaking hands with her grandfather as if he wasn't plotting the innocent old man's ruin. Seeing the spark in her grandfather's eyes, she amended that. He scented an advantage to be gained and he was summoning up the blarney. Nick smiled at her, his eyes grey as slate and just as impervious.

'Markham Cole.' Discreetly elbowing himself in front of his rival, Markham shook Nick's hand vigorously. 'We met at the French Embassy a couple of months ago, remember? I've been thinking that we might be able to do each other a little favour...had something in mind for a little while that you might be interested in. Maybe we could get together one day this week for lunch...'

'No!' That slipped out before she could stop it and Maggie found herself the cynosure of three pairs of eyes, two puzzled and annoyed and one cynically amused. 'I mean, don't you know it's rude to wade right into business when you've just met someone—— ?'

'Oh, I'm all for going straight to the point,' Nick Fortune murmured silkily, and Maggie felt what little control she had over the situation rapidly slipping out of her paralysed grasp. Oh, God, no...he was going to blow the whistle on Finn. In their current mood that was all the grandparents would have needed to be back at each other's throats, and all Finn's hopes for a bright future for Donovan & Cole would be down the drain.

'Yes, well, I'm sure that doesn't mean we can't observe the social amenities,' she said stiffly, thinking with an inward groan that she sounded like some sour-faced old dowager.

'What's the matter with you, girl? You never complained before.' Even her insensitive grandfather noticed her poker-like rigidity. 'Never had time for any of that social stuff when she was a kid. Bit one of her governesses once, when the woman tried to make her wear a dress. Nearly took her finger off. Cost me a mint to buy her out of that one.'

'Paddy!'

'Well, it's true. You were a real biter in those days, a real scrapper.' He sighed with a nostalgia that Maggie thought was misplaced, considering that she realised now that a lot of her 'scrapping' had been to do with trying to make up to Paddy for not being born a boy. 'You take my advice, Fortune, don't get too close to those pearly whites.' He chuckled. That was Paddy's heavy-handed idea of a joke.

Nick smiled enigmatically. 'Once bitten, twice shy.' Only Maggie understood the depth of mistrust in that statement. She swallowed, deciding that she might as well

take the bull by the horns. There was no point in standing
here and letting him draw out the agony.

'Why are you here, Mr Fortune?'

'I thought we'd decided it was Nick.'

'Old Nick, more like,' she muttered under her breath,
her brown eyes melting with fury.

'Old enough to know better, certainly.'

Her temper snapped. 'Did you come here just to utter
cryptic mumblings, or for a reason?'

'A very good reason. To see you.'

'Nick!' There was a world of familiarity in that furious cry and Maggie cursed herself as their audience was
alerted.

'Here, you two ain't up to something, are you?'

'Paddy!'

'Well . . . this talk of separating come out of the blue.
You treading toes, boy?'

Maggie blanched at the challenge. And to call Nick a
boy. Nick, who could crush her grandfather, and
Markham, too, with one hand tied behind his back. She
waited fatalistically for his furious comeback. His eyes
were shading into hazel now, she noticed, giving him a
shrug of weary resignation. Had she known it, the vulnerable curve of her mouth revealed a hint of relief at
the thought that all the deception would soon be over.
For once Maggie was tired of the game, of fighting and
being a pillar of strength.

'Are you questioning my honour?'

'Er . . .' The steely quietness of the question unnerved
Patrick, who specialised in competing against roar and
bluster.

'Or is it the lady's honour that you impugn?'

Impugn. Maggie could see Paddy turning the unfam-
iliar word over in his mind.

'That's about your level, isn't it, Donovan? Calling
your own granddaughter a faithless slut!' Markham
played to the advantage. 'Don't you fret, Maggie, dear.

I don't believe a word of it. If your grandfather wasn't senile he wouldn't either.'

'You're the one calling her a slut, Cole—you always were a foul-tongued snake under that namby-pamby front. I was just asking, Maggie. A man can ask, can't he? I'm worried about you. You're looking too thin.' Sam, are you listening? Maggie thought hysterically. 'And jumpy. You ain't highstrung, Maggie, you got the Donovan nerves, but anyone can see you're fretting about something.' He brightened suddenly. 'Maybe it's hormones. You pregnant, Maggie?'

'Pregnant?' Markham temporarily forgot his hostility at the suggestion, his face was wreathed in smiles. 'Maggie, are you...?'

'No! No, of course not!' She hurried on in case someone asked, why 'of course'? 'It's my diet, that's all. Lots of coffee, it makes me nervy. Do we have to air the family linen in front of a stranger?'

'Nick's not a stranger,' Paddy made up for his unfortunate suspicions by clapping the younger man on the back. 'Nick's got a girl of his own, he understands the strains of parenthood. Besides, when you do business with a man, it's a good thing to know something about his background, right, Nick? Dinner, tomorrow night, how does that sound? Markham here has a few good ideas, I'll admit, but he's behind the times. He's old-fashioned. It's his grandson that wields the power now, and Finn and I get on like a house on fire...'

To her bewilderment and dismay the three men began discussing deals, Markham and Patrick competing for Nick's attention. Soon they were drinking whiskeys, ensconced around the desk, leaving Maggie to seethe with helpless fury. Couldn't they see, the doddering old fools, that he was just stringing them along, encouraging them to snipe and bluster at each other? If it hadn't been so terrifying it would have been funny, the two deadly enemies falling over themselves to court a third, common to them both. She had to warn them, but first she had to get rid of Nick. He obviously wasn't ready to make his move yet, was still paying out the rope. Maybe there was still time to escape the noose.

However, events took an even more treacherous turn when the conversation happened to touch on the success of the new Fortune jewellery and Nick's mention of an exclusive, top-of-the-line designer who had just produced a number of yet-to-be-released pieces that were to be marketed internationally.

'How about that, Maggie? You've got a birthday coming up in a few weeks. How would you like a few baubles? When can we buy one of these things, Nick?' Paddy asked eagerly. Maggie could see that he thought he could kill two birds with one stone—placate Maggie and snare Nick's goodwill at the same time.

Of course, Markham wasn't about to let the opportunity slide by, either, and neither man was going to let the fact that the pieces weren't going to be put on general sale defeat them. They dug their heels in, and soon an unofficial auction was taking place.

'This is ridiculous,' Maggie broke in when the bidding began to get aggressive. 'I don't need any more jewellery. And anyway, you can't buy the stuff sight unseen.'

'Diamonds are diamonds,' protested Paddy stubbornly. 'And Nick wouldn't sell me a dud. He has a reputation to uphold.'

'Finn hinted that you wouldn't say no to a pair of earrings,' said Markham. 'And if there's a bracelet to match you can't break up the set. Not diamonds, too cold for your colouring. You need rubies...and emeralds.'

'But I don't like emeralds. Besides, it's not the gift, it's the thought that counts.'

'Well, you can see how much we're thinking about you, and it's not even your birthday yet!' her grandfather pointed out cunningly. The two of them arguing was bad enough, but Maggie suddenly had a nasty premonition of the reign of terror that could ensue if the two old reprobates ever got together. Individually they were fairly formidable...together they would be unstoppable!

'And here's the man right here who can give you a preview. You could do that, couldn't you, Nick?' Markham asked. 'Maggie could pick out what she liked and you can bill me.'

'Me! I'm the one who's buying,' said Paddy fiercely.

The brief altercation was soon over, with Nick suggesting that Maggie choose several pieces and the protagonists pay half each. The solution was grudgingly accepted, but Maggie could see the brooding and plotting. She had a feeling that she was going to come out of this with the whole store!

'Look, it's not that I don't appreciate your thoughtfulness,' she protested, knowing full well it was their rivalry rather than their love that was governing their generosity, 'but, really, I just want something simple——' Nick's gleam of scepticism annoyed her.

'Then you'll appreciate what Sanchez has done, he specialises in stylistic simplicity. In fact...' the lush, dark lashes swept down to veil the expression in his eyes as he checked the watch at his wrist—no elegant advertisement for his brand but a plain, rugged, well-worn instrument which suited the personality of its wearer to a T '...they'll be available at a security check later on this evening...perhaps you'd like to see them before anyone else has a chance to bid. I expect most of these pieces to go through private negotiation... In fact, why don't you and your husband be my guests for dinner? Then we can go on to the vault and you can take your pick.'

'Finn's not here,' Maggie admitted unwillingly. 'He's in Wellington. Won't be back until tomorrow.'

'Oh, really?'

By now Maggie was heartily suspicious. From that mocking murmur Nick knew damned well Finn wasn't around. He was probably having her husband followed.

'What a pity. Because some of the collection is due to be shipped out tomorrow...' He trailed off regretfully.

'Yes, well, that's the breaks,' said Maggie, not quickly enough, for Paddy had responded with his usual alacrity to the challenge.

'Now, there's no reason that Maggie can't go along. Finn won't mind. You can choose something from him, too. You can't turn the man down, Maggie, not when he's put himself out to make the offer.'

That was what she was afraid of.

'I wouldn't want to be accused of compromising your granddaughter by being seen dining with her alone...' There was just a slight tinge of irony in there, enough to push another of Paddy's buttons.

'Now, now... I insist. You're a friend of the family; why shouldn't you two have dinner? In fact, I think it's a great idea. Take your mind off...whatever it is, Maggie. In fact, why don't *I* make the arrangements? The dinner can be on me, as a kind of apology for any offence I might have inadvertently given.'

Markham began to breathe heavily, seeing himself out in the cold, but Nick defused the moment with infuriating ease. 'I wouldn't dream of it. After all, I'm the one who's going to profit from the evening, to quite a considerable extent...'

Maggie shivered. She had the feeling he didn't mean financially. She tried to dredge up an impeccable prior engagement, but against three determined men her protests were sunk before they had even set sail. All Maggie could hope to do was to hustle the two old men out and fling a bald refusal at the serpent of temptation.

'You know why they don't mind my being seen with you, don't you?' she snapped when the bickering grandparents had departed, after separately whispering that they would talk later about what had initially prompted their visit. 'It's because they're trying to butter you up and they hope to use the fact that you've publicly associated yourself with the family.'

'Which family? Montague or Capulet?' Nick didn't rise to the bait. 'Are they always like that?'

'Today was one of their good days. I'm not having dinner with you, Nick, so you can wipe that smug expression off your face.'

'Scaredy cat.'

The childish taunt threw her. 'Don't think I don't know what you're up to.'

'Oh, and what am I up to?' said Nick, touring the room, picking up ornaments, studying the sophisticated sound and audio equipment that made it more an entertainment centre than a library.

That was the big one. She took the fight into his territory. 'You've been buying up shares, haven't you? You've started buying Cole and Donovan shares. Why?'

'You tell me. You seem to be the one with all the answers.'

Didn't she wish.

'People have noticed, you know. You won't be able to hide behind your nominee companies much longer. Don't imagine for one minute that you'd succeed in a hostile takeover——'

'Perhaps I don't want to take over. Perhaps . . . at the appropriate time, I'll dump the shares and run.'

Thereby causing a crash. 'That sort of thing is illegal!'

'I don't see any witnesses, do you?' he taunted, looking around. 'Besides, what makes you think I'm the one behind the buying?'

'Because you're gloating, that's why. Look, Nick, you saw what Markham and Patrick are like . . . they're old men, for goodness' sake, they put their lives into those companies. You can't destroy what they've built just on some vengeful whim . . . think of all the people who work

for those companies. A lot of innocent people will suffer,
just for the sake of your pride——'

'It's more than pride, Maggie, and you know it. You
had ample warning.'

'A week——'

'In which your husband has done nothing to dis-
courage Laurie's infatuation. If you *really* want to know
what I'm planning...' He paused tantalisingly, and she
tapped her foot impatiently in the thick pile of the rug,
maintaining an air of spurious hauteur. 'I'll tell you over
dinner,' he went on.

'I told you, I'm not going.'

'Fine.' He turned, catching her by surprise with the
ease of his acquiescence. As he strode out of the door
he tossed over his broad shoulder, 'I hope you like surprises, Maggie!'

'Wait! Nick—wait!' He made her run after him. Her
heels clattered over the slate tiles as she caught him by
the door. 'Damn you, Nick, this is blackmail!'

'How shocking.'

She chewed her lip. 'Why do you *really* want me to
come to dinner?'

'Perhaps *I* perceive an advantage in being associated
in public with the family...'

'You make us sound like the Mafia.' She scowled.

'The way those two carry on they'd fit right in. Family
honour seems to loom rather large in their lives...I
wonder how they'd treat anyone who'd besmirched it?'

Was that a threat? She made a decision. 'All right,
I'll have dinner with you, providing you promise to listen
to reason...'

'I always do.'

She sniffed. At that moment Sam staggered out from
the direction of the kitchen, eyes streaming. Maggie instantly forgot the smug devil before her.

'Oh, Sam, I'm sorry. I really didn't mean it about the chilli. I'm going out to dinner, anyway. Sam ... are you OK?'

He wiped his eyes, nodding as she patted him consolingly.

'I'm such a witch. You made me feel guilty and I took it out in temper ... but I really didn't mean it. I'm so sorry, Sam. Forgive me?'

'Sure.' Sam's voice was thick, but not with tears as he dried his wet cheeks on the frilly apron that only emphasised the masculinity it adorned. 'Lucky I hadn't started the chilli, then ... I'll use the onions in a Spanish omelette for myself.'

'Onions?' Maggie suddenly registered the eye-stinging aroma. 'Why, you ... you enjoyed making me grovel, didn't you?'

'Made my day,' Sam grinned. He blinked red eyes at the man by the door. 'You going out? What shall I tell Finn if he rings?'

Finn never bothered to phone when he was away—at least, not Maggie, at any rate. It was just Sam's way of warning her. He might not be privy to the secret of her marriage, but Maggie had the feeling that he had guessed most of it, and they had spoken freely to him about the upcoming divorce and the need for the utmost delicacy.

Conscious of the disapproval beating at her, she laughed. 'Tell him I'm out seeking my fortune!'

CHAPTER SIX

Two hours later, as Nick ushered her into the restaurant, Maggie was already regretting her flippant approach to the ordeal ahead. The restaurant was Italian, homely, a tiny neighbourhood place bulging at the walls with casual diners. Others hung around in the foyer, waiting for take-away orders. For a heartbeat Maggie felt embarrassingly uncomfortable, aware of being sinfully overdressed as people turned to stare. She hadn't felt so socially disadvantaged in . . . well, ever.

In consequence she gave the dark-eyed waiter who arrived to show them to a hastily reset table a dazzling smile. Damn Nick Fortune...minus the tie which he had left in the car he looked perfectly at home in his grey suit and open-collared silk shirt. It was his revenge, of course, for having been left to cool his heels for a good ninety minutes while Maggie 'nipped upstairs for a wash and brush-up'. She had luxuriated in a hot bath and taken her time washing her hair and doing her face and nails before sliding into a slinky black Oscar de la Renta cocktail dress. She had teamed it with strappy high-heeled shoes in pink satin and Isabel Canova's long pink silk evening gloves with tiny black ants on them. Dressed to the teeth she had felt equal to anything, but she had underestimated Nick.

He had been on the phone when she had sauntered back into the library, nursing a scotch and deeply immersed in business. He hadn't said a word about the length of time she had kept him waiting, and he had paid her a bland compliment on her appearance with every appearance of sincerity. She ought to have suspected something then. Nick Fortune wasn't a man to turn the other cheek to a slight. So, instead of taking her to the kind of elegant establishment she was used to, he had brought her here.

'I suppose I should be grateful you didn't bring me to a truck stop,' she said wryly.

'You should,' he agreed coolly. 'But I didn't see the need to sacrifice my palate to make a point. The food here is excellent, even if the surroundings leave something to be desired.'

She shrugged. 'I'm not a snob.'

'Yes, you are. You tried to put me in my place because I'd dared to cross you. And it never occurred to you to ask where I intended to take you. You dressed to intimidate, to deny me a choice. You wanted to meet me on your own ground, in elegant surroundings where you hoped to make me feel inferior.'

'I did not.' She was genuinely bewildered at the deep reading of what had essentially been a rash, ill-considered act of defiance.

'No?' He didn't believe her, his smile irritatingly smug.

'No! I didn't want to go *anywhere* with you, if you'll remember. You forced me into this, and if you don't like it you can lump it! You're lucky I didn't order Sam to kick you out.'

'He would have had his work cut out.' The silky voice revealed its hard edges.

'Sam is a karate black-belt.'

He said nothing, and his silence dismissed the threat as negligible. Maggie glared at the salt-streaked black head tilted over his menu. He glanced up and caught the glare.

'Don't feel so much like laughing now, mm, Maggie?' He had no intention of letting her know that he had admired the way she had shrugged her embarrassment off, with the natural grace of one capable of *making* herself feel at home wherever she might be. It confirmed

something else that he had already sensed about
her...that under that frivolous socialite lurked a far more
complex woman...a core of strength, a little rusty
perhaps from lack of use in her pampered life, but there
all the same. Suddenly she did it again—surprised
him...for she laughed.

'I got you mad, Nick, you have to admit that! I wasn't
sure, with your being so cool and polite. But I got you
real mad!'

He acknowledged her victory with a little tilt of his
head. 'I don't like being kept waiting. Remember that.'

'I would rather have liked to try a truck stop,' she told
him. 'I love hot dogs and hamburgers and all that junk
food. Sam won't have it in the house, and I swear he
can smell a hamburger on someone's breath at twenty
metres.'

'Sam and his...abilities and preferences...seem to
loom rather large in your life. You seem to have a
very...close relationship with your staff.'

'Now who's the snob?' teased Maggie, ignoring the
obvious opening. If Nick Fortune wanted to know anything, he could damned well stoop to *asking*.

'Is he your lover?'

She hadn't really expected him to ask. The people she
knew usually skated delicately around the subject.

'Is that why your husband needs to publicly reinforce
his masculinity? Because he's been castrated at home?'

The urge to smack him across the face was very strong.
She clenched her gloved hands in her lap. He was needling her deliberately in order to gain the advantage. The
trouble was that she couldn't think of anything appro-
priately cool and cutting to reduce him to size. Her face
froze into a pale, haughty mask as she inwardly
floundered.

Nick leant forward and continued in a tone of abrasive
interest. 'I suppose a woman like you would need

someone very skilled and inventive in bed. Is Sam as good as he looks?'

'Nick!' She cast hasty looks at the adjacent tables and let out a shaky breath through smilingly gritted teeth. 'You really are incredible...'

'So I've been told.' His slitted smile gave the murmur a heated implication. 'And you're blushing. Am I embarrassing you, the sophisticated merry wife of legend? I thought this kind of banter was meat and drink to your set...'

'*My set* goes more for subtle wordplay than...than...'

'Honest statement?'

Maggie sternly opened the large plastic menu and scanned it with unseeing eyes. 'Talking of meat and drink...'

'Hiding, Maggie?'

'Hungry, *Nick*.' She imitated his taunting tone but refused to lift her eyes. On the periphery of her vision she could see that her blush had sunk to her chest, and there was a great deal of it revealed by the plunging, figure-hugging neckline of her dress.

'You've only yourself to blame for that.' Satisfied that he had thoroughly routed her, he studied his own menu, his mouth twitching at the waves of hostility thickening the atmosphere. He was enjoying himself. Each time he rattled her she was a little slower to recover. He had the feeling that Maggie Cole was used to handling recalcitrant males with ease. That made his ability to fluster her all the more intriguing, not to mention flattering to his ego. 'If I feed you, will it improve your temper?'

'I don't have a temper... at least I didn't until I met you.'

'You mean you've never really needed one up until now. You've always had everything exactly your own way.'

'And I plan to continue doing so,' said Maggie bravely, snapping the menu shut now that she was sure her unaccustomed blush had faded. 'I'll have *tortellini* first and then *osso buco*,' she told the young waiter, hovering uncertainly by their table, attempting to pretend he wasn't fascinated by the conversation.

He scribbled down her order and then Nick's and then began to fill their glasses from the iced-water jug on the table. As he did so he slid a sidelong glance at Maggie and murmured something in Italian under his breath. Fortunately it was highly complimentary and Maggie couldn't resist sweetly thanking him in impeccable Italian, her dark eyes glowing with a sultry light. The young man was predictably flustered, and Maggie was repaid by a light dousing of icy water from his trembling hand. The poor boy exploded in a flood of remorse, practically crying as he tried to mop up the result of his momentary inattention. Only Maggie's laughing assurances that the dress could do with a wash calmed him down.

A little more Italian and coy, silent hints that it was a privilege to be served by such a fine specimen of manhood sent him on his dazed way, pride restored.

'Is there anyone you can't wind around your little finger?' asked Nick drily, when order was restored.

'Not so far,' she told him boldly, her spirits revived by the ridiculous incident.

'The dress is silk, isn't it? Will there be a watermark?'

Maggie shrugged.

'If there is you must let me replace it.'

She couldn't take him seriously. 'It's one of a kind.' *Like you.* No one else of her acquaintance would have bothered about a ruined dress. Dresses, like lovers, were considered to be disposable, no matter how expensive.

'It wouldn't have happened if I hadn't brought you here.'

Good. He was feeling guilty. 'You're right. You owe me.' She saw with amusement that she had taken him by surprise. He had expected a polite demur?

'How much?' She could see him mentally getting out his cheque-book.

'A lot. But I'll take it in kind.'

'Oh, really?' Something sparked in the back of his eyes, and she hurried to disabuse him.

'In shares. Cole and Donovan shares.'

He leaned back in his chair. 'Clever.'

'Going to renege?' she taunted him.

'Yes.'

Of course. 'You're no gentleman.'

'I thought you'd decided that already.'

'I wasn't sure.'

'Well, now you know.'

There was a small silence while they stared measuringly at each other. Maggie hadn't really expected it to be that easy, but she couldn't rid herself of a vague sense of disappointment.

'You do have the shares, though, don't you?' she insisted.

'I have a very extensive portfolio. My investment manager handles the details.'

'Now who's hiding?'

'Everyone has something to hide. What's your secret?'

She had so many she wouldn't know where to begin! 'You said you were going to tell me what you were planning——'

'And so I will. But not on an empty stomach.'

'I warn you, Nick, you can't put me off forever. I'm not going to take no for an answer.'

To her astonishment Nick actually fluttered, like a girl, 'Maggie, I—I think we at least ought to get to know each other first...'

Her *tortellini* had arrived, along with the mournful silent reproach of the waiter. Maggie could feel herself beginning to blush again as she realised the connotation that he must have put on the conversation. She fumed in silence, ignoring Nick's grin, until the boy had left.

'I really ought to walk out——'

'Then you'll miss the opportunity to worm any information out of my unsuspecting innocence,' he told her calmly, already enjoying his *antipasto*.

'Innocence, my eye,' Maggie scoffed. 'I bet you lost that the day you were born!'

'Oh, I was stubborn, it took a little longer in my case. I had to have it knocked out of me.'

'You mean, in the boxing ring?'

He looked at her for a moment, as if debating whether to continue the verbal games. 'No. At school. I was small until I was twelve or so and I was a bastard...both crimes in the narrow little streets where I grew up. I learned early on that to ignore a taunt was to ask for a beating. So I learned to handle myself...and others. And then I had to learn to handle the reputation I acquired...always some hotshot wanting to try his luck.' There was no boyishness in the grin and Maggie felt a pang for the boy who never was. She lowered her eyes so that he could not read the vulnerable impulse to comfort. He would despise her compassion. She took refuge from the unwelcome ache in her throat by sheathing compassion in callousness.

'So the vanquished became the victor. Were you the school bully?'

His face hardened. 'I never started fights, I only finished them. And I never picked on anyone smaller than myself. It was the law of the jungle, the survival of the fittest.'

And, oh, how he had survived. But at what price?

'And how did your mother feel...having to patch up all your battle scars?' Both proud and despairing...the way that Maggie felt for him? Relieved that even in the jungle he had retained the dignity of personal honour, was capable of mercy towards someone ill-equipped to combat his brute strength. Someone like Maggie...

'My mother didn't know the half of it. She had enough to cope with without worrying about my problems...earning enough to eat for a start.'

'Didn't your father pay any support?'

He smiled at her naïveté. 'The kind of man who runs out on his pregnant girlfriend isn't likely to be meticulous about keeping in touch.'

'Oh.'

'My mother never told me who he was, and I didn't ask. It was enough that he abandoned her when she needed him—after her parents had turned their backs on her shame. My mother was decent, hardworking and dirt-poor all her life. She made one mistake, and, oh, how she was made to pay for that mistake. She died when I was sixteen, just starting to earn enough in the boxing ring to free her from the drudgery of cleaning other people's toilets.'

The crudeness was a gauntlet between them and Maggie was shocked, but not in the way he had intended.

'At sixteen? Did they allow that?'

'I lied about my age and who I was. I was good enough to make the illegal circuit where the *real* money was made. Where Queensberry was a pub, not a set of rules, where only cowards fought with gloves on.'

The battered face now made sense. Maggie's eyes darkened stormily. 'You could have been killed.'

He shrugged, searching her face for the strange fascination that many of the society women he had met felt for his raw, brutal past. Violence seemed to excite something deep inside them. It was that which had drawn Delia to him. But once her curiosity had been satisfied she had claimed to be repelled by his 'gorilla mentality'. In Maggie's face there was only anger.

'It happened. And I was lucky. I'd only been on the circuit for a while when I was seen by a boxing promoter who wasn't just out for a fast buck. He put me into training until I was old enough to qualify for the legit-

imate professional ring. He channelled all my rage into
something more constructive—ambition. And he was
generous enough to show me that there was a world
outside the ring that I could also take by the tail if I
cared to. I found that money and success could buy what
was denied me by the circumstances of my birth.'

'Respectability?' she guessed, thinking about his plans
for Laurie.

He laughed. 'Power.'

'And now that you have it ... is it everything you
thought it would be?' she asked curiously.

He looked at her, the beautiful woman sharing his
table, the woman he had coerced into his company and
whom he had intended to frighten the daylights out of.
He smiled.

'And more. . . .' He leaned back as he watched her un-
selfconsciously dig around in her veal knuckle for the
precious marrow that gave *osso buco* its richness. What
an odd combination she was. She took his intimate rev-
elations—things he hadn't even told his friends, let alone
his enemies—in her stride and, in spite of the fact that
they were on opposite sides of the fence, he couldn't
shake the conviction that she would never use the
knowledge against him. The certainty filled him with
unease. How did she do it? She was out of the self-same
mould as Delia—what made her any different? What
made him hesitate to crush her?

As he watched she licked her lips and the innocent
eroticism of the gesture sent a powerful jolt to his loins.
He straightened, unease deepening. To force his mind
back to the task in hand he began to ask the kind of
probing, intrusive questions that should have instantly
set her back up. But to his frustration Maggie Cole
proved shatteringly trusting, just when he'd wanted her
to stand up and fight. She told him cheerfully about the
feud that had set Coles and Donovans at each other's
throats. She happily admitted that she had been the wild

brat her grandfather had accused her of being, unknowingly painting a picture of splendid isolation that intrigued her listener, especially when the word 'we' began to creep into the telling of her naughtier escapades.

'Who's we?' he enquired when she told him of an incident that had put her off smoking for life.

'Oh, F—a friend,' she stammered, suddenly looking guilty.

'A boy, of course,' he said, cynically judging the reason for her guilt.

'Well, yes...'

'A friend of the family?'

She dabbed her lips with a napkin to gain some time, wondering why the easy lie didn't rise easily any more. 'Not a *friend*, exactly,' she said vaguely, her eyes sliding away from his.

Incredibly, he made the quantum leap in imagination from the single clue of the unconscious emphasis on *friend*. 'An enemy, then.' A single beat. 'Finn? You and Cole were friends when you were children? *How?* If your grandparents were such implacable enemies?'

Maggie shrugged, lining up her knife and fork on her well-cleaned plate, wondering what else she had given away in her enthusiasm to show him that she wasn't just a cardboard cut-out doll. Hadn't she already learned that behind that battered mask of a face was a shrewd animal intelligence, a natural instinct for finding the truth.

'They never knew,' she admitted slowly. 'Finn and I...we met in the park one day when we'd both escaped our nannies.' A small smile of reminiscence curled across her mouth. 'He stole my bread and pushed me in the duck pond. He was even more of a brat than I was. Then he called me a crybaby girl, so I kicked him in the knee and pushed *him* in.' Her voice was rich with satisfaction and humour remembering the shock on that deceptively angelic face. 'Then the park-keeper came along and yelled at us and we had to run away and hide.

We made a blood pact not to tell. We didn't know each other's names then, and by the time we did it didn't matter . . . in fact, it made our meetings in the park all the more exciting.'

'How long did it go on?' He was fascinated by the play of expressions across her face, careful not to disrupt the flow of memory.

'It never stopped.' Maggie shrugged ruefully. She had come this far, she might as well continue. It might help Nick appreciate Finn as a person rather than as a caricature playboy. 'We always found ways to keep in touch. As far as we were concerned, we were family . . . neither of us had any, you see . . . no brothers and sisters or cousins our own age. I suppose we . . . we fulfilled a need in each other.'

'And no one found out, in all those years?'

Maggie grinned, a leftover from her mischievous youth. 'We were very careful to glare at each other in public and competed to deliver the best snub . . . but when we wanted to talk it was always just the two of us. You've seen the grandparents, the way they carry on—it's always been like that. You can't reason with them—if they'd known about Finn and me they would have found out some way to break us up, even though it was all so *innocent*.'

Nick stroked his wine glass, eyes lowered to hide his rush of elation. For some reason—absurd, considering that the two were now married—the innocence of that boy-girl relationship mattered.

'All these years, they've nursed this hatred along, taken it to ridiculous extremes. I can't believe that whatever happened to spark it off could have been that unforgivable!'

'Perhaps it wasn't.'

'What do you mean?' She looked at him impatiently.

'Perhaps they enjoy it too much to let it go.'

'Enjoy it?'

'They're old men. They've both suffered the loss of almost everyone they've loved—what else have they to fill the empty spaces in their lives?'

'That's ridiculous!'

'Is it? Neither of them married again, although I'm sure the opportunity was there if they had wanted it. They didn't—they preferred to devote themselves to empire-building, but every empire needs the incentive of an enemy to spark its growth. What no doubt began as a very personal feud developed into an institution over the years, a satisfying ritual . . . a security blanket, if you like, something to vent one's feelings under safely. They were certainly enjoying themselves tonight, squabbling over you.'

'You don't know what you're talking about,' said Maggie firmly and then she hesitated, loath to give him a weapon but driven to say, 'They still think that Finn and I met when we were overseas, and I'd prefer to leave it that way.'

He studied her stiff expression for a moment but didn't ask the obvious: why? 'Would you like some dessert, or a liqueur?'

She thought guiltily of the extra pound that had appeared that morning and temporised. 'I wouldn't mind an Irish coffee. Paddy doesn't consider a meal complete without a small slug—it made me feel very grown-up when he started giving me his "special Irish" when I was about twelve. I hated the taste but I persevered in the interest of family honour.'

'An Irish coffee, then. And after that . . . I think it's time we got down to the business of the evening, don't you?'

CHAPTER SEVEN

NICK FORTUNE nodded to the two poker-faced men in green uniforms and they withdrew silently, pulling the heavy steel door closed behind them. Maggie's nerves tightened as it clunked solidly into place, sealing them off from the outside world. The walk-in vault was large and well-lit, but suddenly it felt oppressively close and intimate.

Nick seemed aware of her inward flutter of panic, if misreading the reason for it. 'A necessary security precaution.' He indicated the seamless door. 'There's air-conditioning in here, so there's no need to worry about suffocation...even if we were to be locked in here all night.'

Maggie shivered as he turned away to the wall of numbered drawers, selecting keys from the heavy ring in his hands. His reassurance had the opposite effect to that intended. *All night*...the evocative phrase sent her mind spinning. What would it be like to spend the long, languid hours of the night in enforced intimacy with Nick Fortune? Her fingers clenched on her pink silk evening purse. Hadn't she already made enough of a fool of herself with her unwary thoughts this evening?

When he had made that remark in the restaurant about getting down to business she had been so ensnared by her angry awareness of Nick that she had leapt to the guilty conclusion that he meant anything *but* business. The shock of forbidden delight she'd felt was so strong that her expression had betrayed her. Nick's smile had been grim.

112

'The *jewellery*, Maggie, I was talking about the jewellery.'

She recovered the aplomb for which she was famous. 'Oh, damn, and here I thought you were ready to spill the beans about your plotting. We have *that* business to settle, too, don't we, Nick?'

'Is that really what you were thinking?' His smile had been a mocking taunt. They'd both known she was lying.

'Of course,' Maggie had said, with sweet, brazen innocence. 'Why, what did *you* think I was thinking?'

She had neatly stolen his initiative and the faint gleam of admiration in his eyes acknowledged it. If he had answered, it would have been *his* forbidden thoughts that he'd have been putting into words and he'd have sounded like an insufferable egotist.

She had forgotten she was facing a man who didn't give a damn about social rules as long as he *won*.

'Does that mean you're not interested in negotiating to become my mistress?'

'I . . . I beg your pardon?' she'd gasped faintly, afraid that she had misheard, or misinterpreted again.

'Of course you're forgiven, Maggie,' he'd said smoothly, making her feel as if she had grovelled on her knees for his kind words. 'I'm flattered, naturally, by your interest and as it happens I currently don't have a lover but, as I've said before, married women don't qualify for consideration. You're a beautiful woman, and I'm sure there must be other men who would welcome being the target of your . . . enthusiasm.' It had all been said in the gentle tone of one trying to let her down lightly. Maggie had been torn between pride and appreciation, rage and laughter. He'd made her sound like a teenager with an impossible crush!

Knowing that to protest would only prolong the provocation, she had retreated into what she'd hoped was a cool, haughty silence, but her eyes had been as black and steamy as the coffee they were served as she'd silently amassed a belated series of crushing retorts.

They had left shortly after for the short journey to the Fortune factory and warehouse, Maggie both eager and treacherously loath to have the extraordinary evening over and done with.

Nick was sliding out a number of the shallow, padded drawers, setting them down on the polished bench that ran the length of one side of the vault.

'Well?' He raised his eyebrows at her and, to prove that she had herself totally under control, she moved to stand beside him, her silk-covered elbow brushing the dark fabric of his suit. As soon as she looked down, Maggie forgot the small electric shocks travelling up and down her arm.

'Oh, how marvellous!' Used as she was to handling beautiful jewellery, Maggie was enchanted. Sanchez had set his stones in lovely, sweeping curves of gold, silver and platinum. The clean, spare lines were a perfect counterpoint to the rich, flashing fire of the voluptuous gems.

'I told you you'd like them.' Nick angled one of the rectangular mirrors on the bench in her direction. 'What would you like to try first? This set perhaps?'

He had a good eye, but Maggie was still annoyed with him. She pointed to something else, a necklace of square-cut emeralds in a very plain gold setting.

'That really needs a woman with less prominent collarbones,' Nick commented knowledgeably.

'I like it,' said Maggie firmly, resisting the urge to clap her hands over the bones in question. She had a good bone structure and had no intention of letting him undermine her self-confidence. It galled her to find out, when she had refused his offer to help put the heavy necklace on, that he was right. Silently she returned it to its drawer and chose another.

'You need a longer neck to wear that one.'

Maggie frowned at her reflection. With the low cut of her gown the wide choker looked all wrong, making her aware of vast amounts of bare flesh. It was *not* because of her neck, she told herself.

Each time she looked at something, Nick made some negative comment but she doggedly continued until she could stand it no longer.

'You know, you're a terrible salesman. Don't you *want* me to find anything I like?'

'You seem to like everything,' he pointed out. 'Which isn't helping you narrow the selection down. At this rate we *will* be here all night...or perhaps that's your intention. Are you trying to compromise me, Mrs Cole?'

'That joke is wearing pretty thin, *Mr* Fortune.'

He grinned and suddenly she could see the cocky young boxer dancing on his feet, ducking every blow while landing telling ones on his opponent.

'Not as long as it gets a rise out of you.'

'I'm shopping for jewellery, *not* a lover. And if I were I'd look for someone with a little more class. It's something money can't buy you, Mr Fortune. You have to be born to it. You have the suit, but it doesn't quite fit. Sometimes it wrinkles and shows its wear.'

His eyes had narrowed at the first insult. 'I'd rather have integrity than class, any day...'

'Your accent is slipping,' she mocked. 'A pity you don't have class *or* integrity. Blackmail, threats and offers of violence aren't exactly the actions of an upright citizen. And no one with any integrity tries to sell his daughter to gain respectability——'

'I'm not selling Laurie!' His outrage bounced sharply off the steel walls of the vault.

'Pressuring her into marrying one of your carefully selected candidates is the same thing.'

'I'm not pressuring her into anything. She's too young to consider marriage at *all*. She needs a little more experience before she is capable of choosing a partner for life.'

'Oh, you mean you want her to sleep around a bit first?'

'No!' His face was darkened with a surge of blood. 'I wasn't talking about sexual experience. I meant *life* experience. She's been very sheltered up until now——'

'And whose fault is that?'

'I said sheltered, not over-protected,' he gritted, holding down his temper with difficulty. 'She has her whole life ahead of her, there's no need for her to rush it.'

'I see. You want her to stay seventeen but *act* like a thirty-year-old. Very logical, Nick. Very realistic. Why cry for the moon when you can have the stars?'

Her sarcasm calmed what her insults had aroused. Nick made an angry sound and rammed his arms across his chest.

'If you're going to pout, Nick, use more lower lip,' Maggie advised him, taking off the earrings she had tried on with fingers that trembled, ever so slightly.

'God, how do I get into these arguments?' Nick asked several million dollars' worth of gems.

'Natural talent,' she told him. 'You're a fighter.'

'I *was* a fighter.'

'You still are.' When he didn't answer she looked at him and caught a fleeting uncertainty in the inward-turned gaze. 'Ashamed of your background, Nick?' she said, deliberately snooty.

He reared automatically, then hesitated. 'Oh, no, you're not going to get me that way again.' His gaze became penetrating, aware. 'You know all the right buttons to push, don't you, Maggie? How much of it did you mean, I wonder?'

'The chip on your shoulder is rather difficult to ignore.'

'You mean that you *would* consider taking a lower-class lover?' he jeered.

'The only barriers to love are the ones that people want to acknowledge.'

'But we're not talking *love*. Does the idea of going to bed with a crude, lusty brute excite you, Maggie?'

'You mean—any crude, lusty brute . . . or *you*?'

She thought he might bite, but he laughed. 'I think we're getting back into dangerous territory here. Having impressed on me my utter lack of class, are you ready to admit that I'm right?'

'About what?' she asked cautiously.

'About this.' He reached for the drawer that he had first suggested.

'Are you sure I'm not too short? Or fat? Or knock-kneed?' She sounded peevish and knew it.

'This will be perfect on you.' He lifted the wafer-thin, intricately-wrought gold necklace with its three teardrop rubies. 'It will enhance your good points and detract from your bad.'

'Good points? I didn't realise you thought I had any,' gabbled Maggie, trying to ignore the brush of his fingers on the nape of her neck, under the thick fall of her hair. Was he genuinely fumbling or was his lingering touch purposeful? He was standing close behind her. She could feel the heat of his body all the way up from her heels to her head. In the mirror she could see the broad, blunt shoulders framing her, the hard angles of his face tautened by his absorption with the unusual clasp.

'Fishing, Maggie?' He had got it at last but instead of stepping back he rested his large hands lightly on her bare shoulders. The thin black straps of her gown suddenly burnt into her skin. What would happen if he moved his hand, if he pushed the strap down and . . . ? She blinked, meeting his gaze in the mirror, her mouth dry at the blatant sensuality of her thoughts. She was unable to utter a word.

Holding her stunned eyes, he moved a hand forward, tracing the path of gold over her creamy skin, down...down to where the ruby tears lay cradled, just above the bodice of her dress.

'You see?' he murmured into her hair. 'Perfect. You have very beautiful breasts, soft and full and round and warm. A jewel, *here*, gives a man an excuse to admire your womanliness without giving offence.' His touch was explicit, a light finger-stroke in the crease where the largest teardrop lay. Maggie held her breath. To gulp in oxygen as desperately as she needed it would be to thrust herself towards his teasing warmth. The lack made her dizzy. Her eyes fell, narrowed beneath trembling lashes as she watched his fingers adjust the two small teardrops on either side of the large ruby so that they lay evenly against their twin cushions of silky-soft flesh.

'One jewel gives a man the excuse to look...three the excuse to linger.'

'W-what if I don't want him to look?' whispered Maggie shakily, her sophistication in tatters.

'Then don't wear a dress like this one. A woman's breasts are still a very potent provocative signal, in spite of the loosening of the inhibitions of the past. A man can admire...and not touch. It's all a matter of self-control.'

Then why wasn't he exercising any? He was still fondling the exquisitely-cut rubies, the hard, uneven knuckles of his powerful hands brushing her tingling skin. There was an odd buzzing in Maggie's ears now and a terrible weakness in her knees that made the support of his chest against her back a necessity. She closed her eyes, a flush spreading over her throat and face as she realised what was cradled against her soft buttocks. His hips were pressing her forward, trapping her against the hard edge of the bench and he had begun a series of tiny rocking movements that shocked her by their suggestiveness. Her eyes flew open and she drew a harsh, gasping breath.

'Nick——'

His eyes rose reluctantly from the erotic contrast of his hand against her breast. At the sight of her flushed face the movements behind her stilled and, as she felt his body tense with shock, she realised that he hadn't even been aware of making them. He had been lost in some wildly erotic dream very similar to her own. She waited for his scorn, his contempt for her and for himself, but it didn't come. Instead he murmured, with the faintest trace of a smile, 'What was I saying about self-control?'

'I don't know,' Maggie murmured huskily in reply, her flush fading along with her embarrassment. He wasn't trying to make her feel ashamed of her arousal, which was as much in evidence as his. She wore no bra underneath the thin black dress and the soft breasts that he had caressingly admired were now taut and thrusting. 'Uh... aren't there earrings to go with this?'

'Mmm, so there are.' It was a moment before he moved his hand to find them.

To her frustration her fingers were now shaking so much she couldn't even find the holes in her ears, much less slot in the gold posts which anchored the ruby drops.

'Here, let me.'

His hands were rock-steady and amazingly delicate for their size. She turned to face him and obediently buried her betraying hands into her hair, lifting it away so that he could see what he was doing. She nearly went through the roof of the vault when he took her earlobe between thumb and forefinger and rubbed it lazily.

'Gently!' he soothed as she yelped at the tugging pain her sudden movement caused. 'I need to find the hole first.'

'Just put it in!' Maggie snapped, and as his mouth quirked she could feel herself going hot all over. 'I meant the earring.'

'Of course you did, Maggie, what else could you mean? I'm sure you're not in this much of a hurry when you're...er...doing other things,' he agreed blandly, finally threading the post through her ear and fastening the butterfly. The other one took just as long. She was aware of being teased now, and struggled to portray the lofty unconcern of a princess putting up with the tiresome but necessary ministrations of a minion.

'There.'

It took Maggie several long seconds of staring at herself before she saw anything but his sensual amusement. 'Oh, yes, they're beautiful.' She turned her head, wisps of hair escaping from her grasp to soften her vibrant profile, admiring the swing of the rubies as they caught the light and glowed with blood-red fire.

'Well, that's one gift settled.'

'Two. Markham can give me the earrings and Paddy the necklace.'

She didn't, he noticed, even bother to ask the price. Maggie Cole would never have to ask the price of anything, gift or no. Any and every whim could be and was afforded. Nick knew what it was like to be considered a rich woman's toy, the kind of woman who had never been told 'no'. However, although Maggie took her wealth and privilege for granted, she didn't appear to trade on it. Unless she was needling him she never appeared callous or uncaring, she was charming to everyone, regardless of their status...and rather *overly* charming with her employee. She gave freely of her time and money, according to a variety of sources, if she considered the object worthwhile. Her enthusiasm for a life which seemed largely devoted to enjoying herself was something he was finding increasingly hard to condemn. Why shouldn't she live the way she wanted, if that way of life harmed nobody and shed warmth and light in places it was needed? In that respect Maggie was the antithesis of Delia, whose main mission in life appeared to have been to make everyone as cynical and discontented as herself. Maggie was a babe in the wood, in comparison. He frowned. Except in her extraordinarily amoral attitude to her marriage...as if respect and fidelity had nothing to do with each other. Her sexuality puzzled him, too, uninhibited and yet strangely unexpressed.

'There's also a ring,' he said deliberately. 'It's not designed to be worn as a set, but it would go well. Perhaps your husband would like to buy it for you.'

She didn't even blink. 'Oh, no, Finn never buys me rings. He knows I don't wear them.'

'Not even a wedding ring?'

She faltered at last. 'Well, he gave me one, of course.'

He looked at the smooth outlines beneath her left glove. 'But you don't wear it.'

She massaged her fingers in that nervous, absent motion that he had noticed before. 'There's not much point, under gloves. No one sees it, anyway.'

'Out of sight, out of mind? That does rather sound like your marriage altogether.' He turned and found the ring before she had time to reply. 'Try it, anyway. I think it's Sanchez' best single piece.'

It was beautiful, the setting almost antique in its solidity and yet not overpowering the central stones, twin rubies entwined in a lover's knot of diamonds. Maggie's face was more wistful than she knew as she shook her head.

'Try it.' His hand slid from her right elbow to her wrist, pushing her glove down with it until the embroidered ants braceleted her slender wrist.

'Don't you ever take no for an answer?' Maggie glared, pulling her arm away.

For some reason that amused him. 'No more than you. What's the matter? Has your weird and wonderful marriage given you some deep-seated psychosis about rings?

I assure you that trying it on isn't going to oblige you to eternal faithfulness.'

She gave up. Under his eyes, taking off her glove suddenly became an alluring act. Because it was close-fitting and she was trying to remove it neatly it took some time. When at last she freed her hand it was immediately swallowed in his. Maggie realised with a shock that it was the first time in a very long while that anyone other than her family had touched her naked hand. Her skin was very soft and sensitive after years of protection from the elements, and the friction of his lightly roughened palm against hers was strange and sensuous.

'You have lovely hands; it's a shame not to show them off,' he said as he slid the ring slowly down her pale slender finger. The unaccustomed weight anchored her hand to his and Maggie stared at the odd rightness of the pairing. The ring fitted her as if it had been made to measure, and she resented the fierce pang of regret she felt. She had thought she was long past all that. Oh, yes, Nick Fortune could cause her pain in all sorts of unforeseen ways, make her ache for things that she couldn't, mustn't want....

'A ring like this makes your hand look even more delicate and pampered and feminine then it is already. Why do you hide under that ridiculous glove fetish?' He turned her hand over and was gently rubbing her heartline with his thumb. 'Do you cocoon your hands from grubby reality the way you cocoon your mind against the ugly reality of your bankrupt marriage?'

He was mocking her again, with that savage undercurrent of distaste. In the circumstances she couldn't blame him for making ridiculous assumptions, but she did. He was so...smug. So sure that he had cornered the market on suffering. He thought that he was the only one who had the guts to conquer adversity, to turn it around ʻo work for him rather than against him. Maggie suddenly wanted to shock him out of his bedrock arrogance. She wanted him to admit that she, too, could handle life's hard knocks. And, less honourably, she wanted to shame him, to see *his* confidence falter.

She calmly removed her hand from his and quickly stripped off her other glove. Then, still holding his eyes with hers, she extended her bare hands in a parody of coyness. Let him flatter her pampered perfection *now*. Pain and triumph mingled in her challenging stare.

Warned by the dark, reckless turbulence within those speaking eyes, Nick didn't look down. He responded in the accepted male manner, taking her hands in his. His steady regard didn't falter as he lifted the hand with the ring and pressed his lips to its smoothness. Maggie's breath caught in her throat as he did the same to her other hand, brushing his mouth gently over the criss-crossed scarring that made her knuckles as battered as his.

'Let go!' There was a hot ache behind her eyes as she tried, too late, to withdraw her betraying challenge.

His reply was to turn her poor, scarred hand over and salute the nerveless palm, his eyes watching her fight for control. 'Have I disappointed you in some way, Maggie?' His breath swirled hot and moist around her defensively half-curled fingers.

It was his challenge now, and she couldn't answer it. 'Let me go.'

'After you gave yourself to me so dramatically? I wouldn't be so cruel. What did you expect me to do? Faint in horror? Cringe away in revulsion? Did you hope I would prove myself that crass and insensitive? That stupid?'

Yes...yes...*yes*! She had wanted to feel nothing for him but a fine contempt. The ache behind her eyes became a fierce sting. As she watched, he raised her hand in his gentle, inexorable grip and slowly kissed each of her unevenly thickened fingers. Only then did he look at the damage. There was no shock, no dreaded pity, no frantic search for the diplomatic thing to say.

'How did it happen?'

'Hot fat . . . a fire,' she found herself saying helplessly. 'When I was eleven.'

'Does it still cause you pain?'

Maggie shook her head. 'There's a bit of numbness, but I still have almost complete use of my fingers. They had to repair some nerves and tendons and do a lot of grafting, but I guess you can say the damage is mostly cosmetic now.'

'Plastic surgery?'

She smiled faintly, without bitterness. 'This is as good as it gets.'

His eyes were the colour of sun-warmed slate as they studied her proud face. 'Is it medically advisable that you wear a glove, or is that just the Maggie style—to flaunt a flaw as a delicious eccentricity?'

'Oh, definitely the latter,' she drawled, recovering her self-possession. What was done was done. What was the point of regretting it? 'It protects public sensibility and means that I don't have to put up with sidelong glances and awkward questions.'

'Tiresome I could understand. But . . . awkward?' He immediately noticed the oblique evasion. 'Exactly what *were* you up to when it happened, Maggie?'

'We were cooking chips in a can over a campfire. We had a fight over who was supposed to be in charge, and push got to shove and . . .' a rueful shrug ' . . . it was my own fault for being so certain that *I* should always get my own way.'

From that familiar expression of open affection Nick knew who her companion had been. His shoulders tensed as he fought the flood of angry outrage that the thought of Finn Cole always evoked.

'Cole pushed you into the fire?' he interrogated harshly.

'No! I told you, we were both nudging and shoving. I decided to prove I could do everything without his help, and the can spilled. We didn't have any water with us, so Finn had to smother the flames under his arm. He still has a little scar there himself.'

'My God, you mean your hand caught *fire*?' For the first time Nick betrayed a shocked revulsion, but Maggie knew instinctively that it was the mental image he was recoiling from, not the physical reality. His fist almost entirely encased her hand as he held it to his broad chest, and she felt a melting tenderness as she absorbed the fierce, unsteady beat of his heart.

'I wouldn't let him run and get help,' she continued, still trying to absolve Finn. 'I didn't want anyone to know he was involved, you see. I was in shock, I think, because I wasn't feeling much pain at that stage, so neither of us thought it was too bad. We had our bikes with us and I let Finn double me home as far as the gates.' She grimaced. 'If Paddy had found out that it had been a Cole who had been sole witness he would have gone berserk. He wouldn't have cared who was to blame or how much Finn had helped, he would have tried to have him brought up on delinquency charges, or at the very least made sure that we never saw each other again. As it was, when I got better, Paddy gave me absolute hell for being so stupid.'

'I don't blame him!' Nick's statement was the forceful expression of a sympathetic parent. 'So you were the one who got into trouble while Cole got off scot-free!'

'Not entirely. In fact, I think it took Finn longer to get over it than I did...thanks to the macho ethic of the male being the responsible partner of any couple. He thought he should have protected a mere girl better.'

'And so he should have!'

Nick's self-righteous snarl amused her. 'He was only eleven, Nick. And nobody, not even a best friend, got the better of Maggie Donovan in those days.'

'Or even these days, I suspect,' he said drily, his pugnacious air dissipated by her teasing.

'Oh, I've calmed down a lot since then. That was a turning-point in my life because Paddy decided that the only place I'd be safe was in a very well-supervised boarding-school. So I was shipped off to be whipped into a little lady.'

'Only it didn't exactly take,' he murmured. 'Does Cole still feel responsible for scarring you?'

Maggie stiffened. 'If you're asking whether he married me because he was haunted by remorse, Dr Freud, then the answer is no!'

'Then why did he marry you?' he asked smoothly.

'Because it was the only way——' She stopped, aghast at how nearly he had succeeded in plumbing another mystery.

'The only way what? That he could get you into bed?'

The crude taunt backfired. Maggie burst out laughing. Even after five years of marriage Finn hadn't managed *that*! Nick smouldered at her secret amusement, the hard, misaligned angles of his face grating against each other. Maggie bit back her laughter and took off the ring, replacing it regretfully in its place.

'I think I'll let Finn choose my present himself,' she said hurriedly. 'He has excellent taste.' Uh-oh, that didn't go down too well, either. She fiddled about, pulling on her gloves. No one else stared at her the way Nick did, as if he could see the workings of her mind. Thank God he couldn't—he would know what a shambles it was in there. 'Er... I'd better take these other things off...'

'Consider them yours. Wear them home.'

'How do you know that the grandfathers' cheques won't bounce?'

'I know down to the last cent how much they're worth. Besides, they're of the old school, where a man's honour rode on his word.'

His comment brought them full circle. Maggie was jolted by the fact that she had completely lost sight of her mission. Her chin came up in a characteristic gesture of haughty determination. 'What are you going to do with those shares, Nick?'

'What do you suggest I do with them?'

She eyed him savagely. 'Don't tempt me.'

His eyes gleamed. 'What's the information worth to you, Maggie?'

'I've already paid the price—a long, boring evening with a self-righteous prig!'

'You shouldn't lead with your chin, Maggie, not when you're in the ring with an old fighter like me.' He glided a broken fist against the pure line of bone. 'You're liable to get your jaw broken.'

Maggie jerked her head away. 'I can handle it, *old man.*'

'Now you're tempting *me.*' His voice was gentle, but full of warning. 'I'm not some punch-drunk fool ready to fall at your feet the way every other man under ninety seems to. I have certain standards——'

'Yes, I know, you've told me often enough—I don't meet them. Well, you don't meet mine, either, buddy.'

'Then why the melting black eyes and the low-cut dress and the poor-little-rich-girl act?'

'It's not an act!'

There was a bare silence. The vault suddenly felt hot and stuffy again.

'No? How very revealing,' he said softly. 'You want the information...but you want me more...'

Yes. *Yes!* Maggie shook her head violently, the rubies thudding against the jaw that burned from his touch.

'I make you angry, but I also make you feel like a woman, which is more than your husband seems capable of doing. He's a taker and he'll take whatever he can get, whatever people are willing to let him have. But not my daughter. I don't share your childhood trust in his sterling character. I'm going to buy every share I can get my hands on, if it gives me leverage. And if merely holding them isn't enough to convince him to leave Laurie alone, then I'll sell him all the way down the river. I'll make sure that his reputation never recovers. His own grandfather won't trust him with another cent. If you're going to stand by him in this, be very sure, Maggie, that you know exactly why. This time he's the one who's going to have his fingers burnt playing with fire.'

'You'd like me to desert him, wouldn't you?' she demanded shrewdly. 'My God, so much for your puritan views on marriage. You *want* to break us up——'

'I want *you* to know what you'll be letting yourself in for.'

'Well, thanks very much for the warning! Aren't you afraid I'll pass it on to Finn?'

'I'm counting on it. If you can preserve your marriage in spirit as well as in fact, I won't *have* to do anything more. If you leave him——' he shrugged '—it'll just make it that much easier to bring him down.'

'Leave him and go where . . . to you? You'd like that, wouldn't you? It would make your revenge complete,' she accused, in a voice that was raw with hurt.

The negative shake of his head was like a slap in the face. 'I won't come between a man and his wife——'

Her laugh of disbelief cut him off. 'But you *are* trying to break up our marriage——'

'Not in the way you mean.' He moved closer. 'Although I won't deny that if you were free . . .' He looked down into her great dark eyes as he made the clumsy admission, and lost the thread of his argument. Rubies quivered against her throat and her breasts, the perfume of her rose around him like a mist, mingling with the familiar scent of his own arousal. Nick Fortune, who had never known a knockout, was suddenly punch-drunk. His head spun, his body weaved as he caught her smooth shoulders to steady himself. He had to know whether she tasted as intoxicating as memory...

'Maggie...'

She did. But one taste was not enough. His words became a whispered seduction against her skin, an erotic litany that invited her to share his intoxication. 'If you were mine I'd shower you with jewels and you'd wear them and nothing else. I'd lie you on red silk sheets and adorn your lovely body with splendour. What a beautiful setting you would be... a glowing nude with rich red rubies in your ears...' His hands cupped her throat, thumbs setting the heavy earrings in motion. 'And lying lovingly between your breasts...' The warm, rough palms slid down to lift their aching roundness.

'And I would place a jewel here, too...' he murmured dreamily, his hands spanning her waist, his thumbs rimming her navel, tracing it through the thin stuff of her dress. She made a tiny sound, and one hand slid lower, the heel pressing against the apex of her thighs causing an explosion of warmth that made her shudder. 'But here you wouldn't need any adornment, Maggie,' he whispered. 'Here, where the heart of your womanhood lies, a jewel more beautiful and more precious than any mere stone... a *living* jewel, and one that can give such priceless, matchless pleasure. Oh, Maggie...'

He drank the soft groan from her lips and drew her closer, his arms sliding around her arching back, dragging her into him, tucking her between his legs as he kissed her... and kissed her... and kissed her... his mouth as hard and urgent as his body.

In the vault each sound was magnified, each rustle and sigh, each aching murmur, so that when the loud, highpitched buzz began it was like a siren that jerked them apart.

Maggie had to lean against the bench, trembling violently as Nick shook himself out of his stupor and stared at the blinking red light on a panel by the steel door.

'It's the alarm,' he said thickly. 'There's a heat sensor so that when someone's in here the alarm trips over every half an hour. If the code isn't punched in within thirty seconds the main alarm goes off at the police station.'

'Then, for goodness' sake, shut it off!' Maggie said shakily. She could imagine the scandal if the police burst in to find her and Nick practically making love among the millions! She smoothed out the wrinkles in her dress, aware of the tiny vibrations set off by each movement. Oh, God, what must he be thinking of her now...?

She felt a little rush of exhilaration as she saw that the finger punching in the code was unsteady enough to slip, on one occasion prompting a savage curse, but by the time Nick turned back to her he had regained a measure of self-control.

'I'm sorry——'

He wouldn't look at her, and that surprised her as much as the apology. 'For making me feel like a woman?'

The long, thick lashes flickered back, and when she saw the huge black pupils she realised why he hadn't wanted her to see. He was as helpless as she.

'Nick——'

'Don't, Maggie. Don't make it any harder than it is. I lost my head. It won't happen again.'

It was an admission of weakness that only made her admire him more. 'You're as hard on yourself as you are on everyone else,' Maggie said sadly, mourning for her lost innocence. All her life she had waited for a man she could love with all the passion in her nature. But this man didn't want her love, and refused to accept her passion. Wasn't there any way to reach him through the tangled maze they had created?

'I'd better take you home.'

'I can take a taxi,' she offered tentatively.

'Don't be ridiculous,' he growled, ramming the last of the drawers back into its slot. 'I think you can trust me to control my libido when I'm behind the wheel.'

'Pity.'

'Maggie!' His hearing must be acute, she hadn't even realised that she had muttered it aloud.

'All right, all right, I'll be quiet. But just remember this was all *your* idea. I wouldn't be here if you hadn't wanted me to be.'

'Quite.' His terse, slipped elocution eased Maggie's frustration. Nick had told her that he had won all his fights as a professional . . . but then he had never had to fight himself before. Who would ultimately win, the man of rigid principles or the man of deep desire?

'Just answer one more question for me?'

'What?' He paused, an impatient hand on the intercom ready to inform the guard that they wished to leave. His wariness told her that he was expecting another sally on behalf of Finn.

'Do you really sleep on red silk sheets?'

The answer was an inarticulate grunt, but the flush on the back of his neck as he demanded the release of the door was very informative. Nick Fortune had crafted his sensuous fantasy from fact, probably while lying on those very silk sheets. The fact that he had now shared that fantasy with its object made it even more potent. Unless he wanted to discard some expensive bedcovers he was going to find Maggie very difficult to forget. She hoped!

CHAPTER EIGHT

'YOU'RE *what*?' Maggie choked out the classic rejoinder, sending a stream of coffee across the immaculate white tablecloth as she crashed her cup down on to her saucer.

'She said she's pregnant,' said Sam helpfully, as he mopped up. 'Another glass of milk, Laurie?'

The girl shook her head with a weak smile. And she *was* just a girl, thought Maggie sternly. Not too young to fall in love, but definitely too young to be tied down to a baby whose father was still married to someone else!

'But...' Maggie couldn't believe that Finn would be so irresponsible, or Laurie, come to that '... Laurie, *how*?'

Laurie went faintly pink.

'Will you tell her?' murmured Sam ironically. 'Or shall I? It's like this, Maggie: when a man and a woman——'

'Sam, go away! Just because we allow you a certain amount of latitude doesn't mean that you can poke your nose into *every* corner of our business! Don't you have some work to do?'

'I am working. I'm really a spy for the Sunday papers.'

'*Sam!*'

He beat a laughing retreat. The papers! Maggie shuddered with the fun they'd have if this leaked out.

She looked at Laurie, meeting baby-blue eyes that suddenly were all woman. She suddenly felt herself going a trifle pink.

'I had no idea that you and Finn were... well, that you...'

Laurie came to her rescue with a nervous smile. 'We love each other very much. I'm sorry...I...we...well, I won't exactly say that we couldn't help ourselves but all this pretence has been really tough on both of us, and I suppose we needed to reaffirm our love in a *committed* way——'

'A baby is certainly a commitment,' said Maggie drily.

'Oh, that part of it was definitely an accident...'

Maggie rolled her eyes. 'Where have I heard that before?'

'No, I mean, truly an accident,' said Laurie earnestly. 'You know what Finn's like, he's paranoid about putting any pressure on me, he insisted on being responsible for contraception, and he used protection every time.' A rueful shrug. 'I guess we're just one of the small percentage who makes up the failure rate. Poor Finn, he's going to go spare when he finds out.'

'You mean, he doesn't know yet?' Maggie's coffee almost took another journey.

'I only found out myself this morning.'

Maggie was doing rough calculations in her head. 'You must have been sleeping together nearly all along,' she realised.

Laurie looked down, blonde hair slithering forward to screen her face. 'Yes.'

Maggie felt a pang of betrayal—not because her husband had taken a lover, but because her friend of many years...her closest friend...had not confided in her. With a wrench she faced the fact that Finn's loyalty was no longer hers to take for granted. He truly did belong to Laurie. Nothing would ever be the same between them. Oh, they would be friends, the three of them, but from now on Maggie would have to tackle her problems on her own. It wouldn't be fair to any of them if she tried to sustain the closeness of her former relationship with Finn. For all their sakes Maggie would need to stand back, not compete, however unconsciously, with Laurie's right to Finn's full attention.

'Am I acting like a wronged wife?' she asked the bent head across the table. 'Sorry, but it was just such a shock. I mean, here I am, an old lady, and you a kid, and you're more of a woman than *I* can claim to be.'

That brought Laurie's head up, her eyes blue and round. 'You mean, you've never...?'

'Never.' Maggie held the twitching corners of her mouth still. 'What's it like?'

Laurie was laughing and blushing at the same time. 'Spectacular. You ought to try it some time...only not with Finn.'

'Cross my heart.' Maggie smiled. 'But why are you telling me first?'

'To give myself courage, I suppose.' Laurie grimaced. 'Finn isn't going to be pleased.'

They both knew it was an understatement. Maggie had passed on Nick's warning to Finn, and she knew that he was keeping a wary eye, along with a lot of investors, on the ominous rise in Cole share prices. The buying patterns seemed erratic, small parcels of shares being traded to apparently unconnected nominee companies. Only Maggie knew that they *were* connected, that behind the maze of directorships stood one man: Nick Fortune.

Unfortunately the picture was being clouded by the not-so-secret activities of Paddy and Markham, who were also cruising the market like basking sharks, swallowing small percentages of each other's shares, sharpening their wits and their knives in anticipation of an orgy of backstabbing. It was taking all Finn's talent for diplomacy to carry on as if nothing was amiss while behind the scenes he was working frantically to try and consolidate support for himself. The last thing he needed was a bombshell of this magnitude.

'He'll get over it,' said Maggie sturdily. 'Once he gets used to the idea he'll be delighted. The first time he told me about you he said he wanted you to be the mother of his children.'

'Did he?' Laurie's small face melted with a delight that faded as she added, 'But I'm sure he had a more long-term view in mind.'

'And you—how do you feel about it? You're so young, and you have your career...'

'Having a baby won't change those things. I'll admit that it's not the way I wanted it, either, but I like children and I always planned to have several...and don't you think that it might go a little way to reconciling its grandfather to the identity of its father?'

Nick...a grandfather! The irresistibly funny notion revisited her, and Maggie began to giggle. Soon the two women were in fits—Maggie wasn't quite sure whether it was of laughter or tears, or both.

'I mean, it worked for you, right?' said Laurie, wiping her eyes. 'And, as straitlaced as Dad can be, he'll want my baby to have a father.'

That was no straitlaced man that Maggie had encountered in the jewellery vault. Ten days later she was still having trouble sleeping at night, particularly since her furtive purchase of red silk sheets for her solitary double bed. She had known she was buying torture for herself, but the impulse had been almost in the nature of a compulsion. If she couldn't have Nick Fortune in person she could have him in her dreams. She had even permitted herself to fantasise that there might be a twisting road to reconciliation for them all, but now even that fantasy had bitten the dust.

'How are you going to tell him?'

'Who? Finn...or Dad?'

'Both.'

'I don't know. That's why I came to you. I realise that you don't know Dad very well, but at least you can advise me about how to break it to Finn.'

Maggie hastened to comply, hoping that Laurie didn't notice her hot flush. She felt like asking Laurie for *her* advice. How do I go about seducing your father? How do I make him fall in love with me at the cost of his scruples? By conspiring with Finn and Laurie against him she knew that she was wrecking any chance of finding happiness with the man she feared that she was fated to love, but what else could she do? It was too late for the truth to put things right.

They waited together for Finn to come home. In Maggie's experience courage was always best grasped and brandished at short notice, before one had the time to worry about consequences.

Unpredictably, Finn took the news quietly...too quietly. His tanned skin went the colour of skimmed milk and he slid gracefully sideways in the chrome and leather Wassily chair that they had pushed him into. It took Sam, with a hefty slug of brandy, to revive him.

'It's the pregnant woman who's supposed to faint, Finn, not the father-to-be,' Maggie told him, when he had recovered enough to sit upright and stare at Laurie as if he'd never seen her before.

'Finn?' Laurie was regarding him apprehensively, her heart in her eyes.

'My God, Laurie,' he said in a shaken whisper, his eyes stroking across her flat stomach. 'A baby? Us? How?'

Maggie saw Sam grin and open his mouth, and she quickly hustled him out of the room before his humour ruined a precious moment.

Later, when she sought them out, Finn and Laurie seemed to be locked in some beatific haze that would admit no pessimism. There was no need for her to worry, Maggie was told; there was plenty of time. Laurie wasn't quite three months pregnant yet and it would be at least another four weeks or more before it would begin to show. Time enough for panic then. For the moment they would trust in Thomas Ritchie, who was still trying to find a short cut to divorce. Finn and Laurie would just have to ride out the waiting period and hope that they could be married before the baby was born. Maggie thought they were being unrealistically calm about the whole fiasco and said so.

'Illegitimacy doesn't carry the stigma it used to,' Finn told her placidly, 'and whatever happens, I'll be listed as the father on the birth certificate. Legitimacy only starts to cause complications in the law of inheritance, and if Fortune carries out his threat we won't have to worry on *that* score. There won't be anything for the child to inherit!'

'Somehow I can't imagine you living on love and penury,' said Maggie tartly. 'Both of you have lived in luxury all your lives. How on earth will you manage?'

'We can always move in with Grandfather, until I get re-established,' said Finn.

The pregnancy must have turned his brain. 'Providing he hasn't cast you off as well,' snapped Maggie. 'A divorce he might be persuaded to swallow, but *another* pregnant bride...while you're still married to me? Not to mention the fact that if Nick ruins you he takes all of us down with you, Markham included. We might all be scraping for a living. At least you should worry for the rest of us, if not for yourself.' That was grossly unfair, considering his recent harassments, but Maggie had to try and shake his supreme confidence somehow.

'I know that Dad has been coming over heavy but I also know why.' Laurie placed a hand protectively over her belly. 'I'm sure Finn and I will be just as protective of *our* child. Dad doesn't want me to make the same kind of mistakes he did. It might take a while, but once the baby comes I'm sure he will accept the inevitability of Finn and me as a couple.'

'When you're a parent you see things from a different perspective,' Finn agreed. 'You're more tolerant of the crazy things that other parents do.'

Maggie stared at them both in utter disbelief. Finn hadn't been a prospective parent for half an hour, and that of a tiny being that was barely even formed yet, and already he was sounding like an escapee from a family sitcom!

It was there and then that Maggie decided that she was the only participant in the farce sane enough to tackle the situation head on. Let Finn and Laurie wallow in their impending parenthood. She, Maggie, would make sure that their misty optimism was justified.

Her first task was to call Thomas Ritchie and check up on the state of play. His news was not reassuring.

'I've tried all the angles I know,' he told her, 'but if you're still adamant about not wanting an annulment there's no way of getting around the two-year waiting period.'

'For a simple divorce that both of us want?'

'There's no such thing as a simple divorce these days, Maggie. It's not even called divorce any more; it's called dissolution of marriage, and the only grounds on which it is granted is separation—that is, that you and Finn have been living separated and apart for two years. I'm sorry, Maggie, but I've gone through everything very thoroughly and there are no loopholes. Not the discreet kind that you want.'

'Two years,' Maggie repeated numbly.

'I told all this to Finn last week. Hasn't he discussed it with you? He told me to prepare the papers. I have them here for signing.'

'He's had a lot on his mind.' In truth she had hardly seen Finn in the past few weeks. And he, the poor darling, had been prepared to make this sacrifice because he knew she didn't want to upset Paddy and Markham. He and Laurie had been prepared to live in sin for the next couple of years, just to satisfy Maggie's selfish desire to keep up appearances. No wonder Finn had passed out when he learned about his impending fatherhood. And the two of them had *still* acted brave and self-sacrificing, waffling on about modern attitudes to illegitimacy! Maggie's determination strengthened.

'What if we changed our mind about an annulment?'

'But Finn said——'

'Thomas, you're *my* lawyer, too,' she reminded him sternly.

'If there's going to be a conflict of interest——'

'Lauric's pregnant,' said Maggie baldly, and there was a short, telling silence at the other end of the telephone.

'Oh, I see... well, I can get you an order for annulment, on non-consummation grounds agreed by both parties, almost immediately.'

Maggie brightened. 'How immediately is "almost"?'

'The time it takes to file and have the court process the application. Say, two or three months.'

Maggie chewed her lip. 'No good.' Laurie would be visibly pregnant by then. They needed time for one scandal to fade before presenting the world with another... by the world she meant Nick. 'Would it be any quicker in the States?'

'In several of the southern US states all you have to do is produce statements from both parties saying that you've agreed to live separately and apart—in other words that you both agree the marriage is over—before a civil judge, and he can order a divorce. So, yes... it can be only a matter of a day or so.'

'Does Finn know about this?'

She could practically hear Thomas's mental shrug. 'We haven't discussed it because I thought it was purely academic. You said you wanted to orchestrate a natural break-up that wouldn't arouse anybody's suspicions. You vetoed the idea of a quickie divorce that first time in my office, remember?'

Maggie remembered her flippant suggestion that they combine their divorce with a remarriage, and winced. She realised that she had never really given Finn the option. She had wanted it all her own way and, out of loyalty and love and probably a bit of entirely unnecessary guilt, Finn had let her 'orchestrate' their separation the way he had let her 'orchestrate' their elopement. For the first time she faced the unpalatable fact that she was a little jealous of Laurie. The girl had everything: personality, intelligence, a talented career, the love of her life equally in love with her, and now a child to consummate that love.

Maggie's sense of guilt was compounded. She was a spoilt, jealous bitch. She had expressed happiness and support for the couple while at the same time unconsciously holding Finn hostage to an old affection. She had been afraid to allow a quick, clean cut because she was afraid of the subsequent emptiness that she would face. Finn had always been there to rely on, but now she would have to rely on herself. Now she would have to create her own sense of personal security and happiness. She stiffened her backbone. Starting now. For once in her life she would carry an idea through to fruition, taking care of all the tiresome details herself. For once she would be *organised*.

'Thomas . . . have you ever been to Disneyland . . . ?'

Three days later Maggie was smugly anticipating easy success. She had booked flights and accommodation for herself and Thomas—via Disneyland, which she visited every time she went to the States—it had become in the nature of a ritual—had signed affidavits from two consulting gynaecologists and one soon to be ex-husband. And the beauty of it was that Finn, still in an impervious euphoria that had him buying stuffed animals by the sackful, had not the slightest inkling of the wedding present he was about to receive. He had signed his affidavit without even reading it, along with a stack of other papers related to—so he thought—the dissolution of their marriage. Thomas had balked dutifully at this small deception, but Maggie had bulldozed his objections with ease, aided by his sneaking desire to just once thumb his nose at jurisprudence.

When she had told Finn that she had decided to spend a few days at Disneyland he had confirmed her disgust with herself by wearily wishing her a good time. It didn't seem to surprise him that Maggie should take off in the middle of a crisis. Maggie was Maggie, a creature of impulse untrammelled by the everyday hassles that others were burdened with. Laurie's disappointment was less well concealed but she was too well-bred, and too loyal to Finn, to make any open criticism. Only Sam kicked up a fuss—such an unholy fuss that Maggie had to let him in on the secret, bribing him with an offer to double his salary if he came to work for her after the break-up went public. Well, Maggie wasn't prepared to be *entirely* self-sacrificing!

The day before she was due to leave was Maggie's birthday and, as tradition demanded, she and Finn had lunch with Markham and dinner with Paddy. The old men took the opportunity to harangue Finn about the proposed merger, finding all sorts of reasons why it shouldn't now go through, predicting dire consequences if Finn ignored the growing signs of a hostile takeover. Cracks were appearing in Finn's golden patience, and both meals ended in indigestion with Maggie dragging him away before he said anything to cause an explosion. When they got back to the apartment Finn was restless and snapped when Maggie suggested that it was still early enough for him and Laurie to go somewhere.

'For instance? We're not supposed to be seen together in public yet,' he pointed out acidly, pouring himself another drink, giving her newly opened eyes another indication of the pain that the restrictions placed upon him. 'Besides, she's in bed with the flu.'

'The flu? In the middle of summer?'

He gave her a sour look. 'It seemed the least contentious way to explain her morning sickness.'

'Oh. Is it very bad? I thought she was looking rather pale last time I saw her.'

'Bad enough. Dammit, Maggie, I should be there, helping her through this!' He knocked back the drink in one swallow.

'And it's only going to get worse,' Maggie murmured to herself, thankful that she was doing something about it.

Finn gave her another sour look, picking up the bottle again and tilting it recklessly against his glass.

'Look, instead of sitting here and drinking yourself into oblivion, why don't you and Sam go out to a club or something? Take your mind off things.'

'While you and Laurie sit at home?' brooded Finn morosely.

'Your harem can do without you for one night, I'm sure,' said Maggie drily, to jolt him out of his misery. She was sure she could rely on Sam to look after him, and it was ages since Finn had enjoyed the company of another male. She would call Laurie herself and indulge in some girl-talk... or rather woman-to-girl talk, she corrected herself derisively.

With a few drinks on board Finn wasn't too hard to persuade and Maggie went to bed with a clear conscience.

At three a.m. bed was just a memory. Maggie was blinding an officer of the law with all the sweetness her silent rage could dredge up, trying to persuade him not to press charges. 'They're very sorry, officer. They didn't mean to cause any damage, and I've already written out a cheque to the owners, and nobody else was hurt. Can't you just put it down to a case of over-exuberance?'

'Over-something, certainly,' said the grizzled constable, taking in with a jaded, experienced eye the three unsteady figures propped against the wall of the police station.

'Well, yes, as I said, officer, they're very, very sorry,' Maggie persisted, adding in a gritty voice that made the tired eyes smile, 'And if they aren't they soon *will* be!'

It took a bit more fast footwork before they were released and Maggie shepherded her charges towards her BMW.

'I'm sorry, Maggie——'

Maggie glared at Sam's single open eye. 'Get in, Sam.'

'Thanks, Mags.' Finn contrived to look forlorn in his ripped shirt, the strapping that supported his cracked collarbone very white under the car park floodlights.

'Shut up and get in.' She turned to the last figure.

'My car is back in town...'

'And it's going to stay there,' she told Nick Fortune flatly. 'That policeman only let you go after *I* promised to drive you home.'

'I could get a taxi.'

'No taxi-driver in his right mind would give you the time of day. Do you even have your wallet?'

Nick frowned vaguely. 'It's in my jacket.' He looked round, as if he expected to find it hanging on a convenient peg in the car park.

'Which is back at the nightclub. I presume you took it off to fight. Get in.'

Nick looked at the open door, at the two men in the back seat. He scowled. They scowled back.

'Honestly!' Maggie slammed the door shut and opened the front passenger door. 'Get in, Nick, or I'll get that cop back and you can spend a nice night in the cells.'

'You don't have to do this.'

'I know; it's just out of the goodness of my heart.' Not to mention the love lodged there! Nick being meek was a new experience and one she rather liked. He had a cut above his right eye and a split at the corner of his mouth. A sling supported his right arm with its strapped hand and wrist. A broken finger, the doctor had told her, handing over a bottle of painkillers that he said she could use for all three of them.

'Wait until they've sobered up a bit, though, because alcohol speeds up the reaction, and don't give anything else at *all* to Mr Fortune—I gave him a diluted injection when I strapped that finger...the two on either side are badly sprained and he's probably still in quite a bit of pain.'

Judging by the grey seeping into the olive complexion, that was a bit of an understatement, thought Maggie, as she put the car into gear. Damn them, they could have killed each other! She let out the clutch with an angry jerk and the car lurched into motion, drawing groans from the back seat and a muffled grunt from beside her.

'Serves you right!' she told them furiously. 'What on earth do you think you were doing? And at the Roundhouse! Couldn't you have found somewhere more public?' Her sarcasm went down like a lead balloon. A thick silence followed her words. 'How did it get started, anyway?' An even thicker silence. The great male conspiracy at work again.

'All right, don't tell me, then. I don't think I want to know, anyway,' she lied, 'and if I do I can probably read about it in the newspapers. You know, violence is the last refuge of the inarticulate. You'd think that three seemingly intelligent men would be able to settle their differences without resorting to their fists, but I suppose alcohol is a great leveller. A few drinks and you all revert to cavemen. I suppose it's too much to expect that you didn't bandy my name about in public like some...some motorcycle mama up for grabs!'

There were muffled snickers from the back seat before Finn hastened to reassure her. 'Oh, no, we weren't fighting over you, Maggie. It was Laurie, not *you*.'

Of course, Laurie! Why would anyone want to fight over *Maggie's* honour? She went hot with embarrassment at her stupid assumption, praying that they were all so drunk that her slip passed them by.

'If you pinned your favours on me, *I'd* be your champion, Maggie,' Nick leaned over to mutter roughly, as if he had easy access to her most secret thoughts even when his own were muddled. 'I'd beat all comers to carry off the prize. You'd like that, wouldn't you, honey...?'

'What's he saying?' Finn clutched the back of her seat aggressively. 'Is he shooting his big mouth off again?'

'Look who's talking!' Nick turned to sneer. 'You talk pretty big yourself when you have Bruce Lee there to cover your back——'

'You mean it was two against one?' Maggie was appalled.

'I was only trying to break them up,' Sam protested thickly. 'Anything I did was purely in self-defence. They *both* hit me!'

'You were supposed to take Finn out and cheer him up, not get yourselves drunk as skunks and nearly arrested,' said Maggie unsympathetically, and nearly drove off the road when she felt a heavy hand descend on her knee. She tried to push it away with her elbow but Nick was determined and she gave up when she saw the swaggering grin that dared her to say anything. She risked a fearful glance in the rear-view mirror, but fortunately Finn was too sunk in his brooding to notice any front-seat manoeuvring. It was with great relief, as the warm hand began to stray further up her thigh, that Maggie pulled up at the apartment. She had planned on dropping off her two drunks before delivering Nick, but to her despair they seemed baffled by the intricacies of the revolving door that guarded the foyer. They would never in a million years be able to figure out how to get a key in a lock.

'You wait here,' she told Nick severely as she got out.

'Sure, beautiful,' slurred Nick, giving her a meltingly meek look.

'I'll be back to take you home in a minute,' she said, to make sure her instruction sank in.

'Home,' he repeated dutifully. He frowned as she began to shut the door. 'Kiss goodbye?'

Maggie turned her back on temptation and shepherded her charges through the revolving door. Even lowered by drink, Nick Fortune was as sexy as hell. She keyed in the security lock and held open the lift doors, only to find that Nick had shambled in their wake.

She took him back out and returned, but he followed her again, like a lost puppy. And a mongrel at that, with his battered face and tousled hair and buttonless shirt hanging open over his rugged chest. His dark trousers, like Finn's, had their share of scuffs and stains. It must have been some fight!

'I thought I told you to stay put in the car.'

He frowned. 'Did you? When?' He lost interest in the answer, leaning his head back against the wall of the lift and closing his eyes as she debated whether to press the point. Maggie looked at the exhausted, disreputable trio and sighed. At this rate she would be trotting back and forth all night. Maybe she ought to try and sober Nick up first before she dumped him on his doorstep.

It was easier said than done. Finn had a tantrum when she accidentally bumped his shoulder against the lift doors and by the time they got into the apartment he was only fit to stumble away, moaning, to his bed. Sam, his good eye distinctly bloodshot, favoured Maggie with a silly grin as he offered to make coffee, but since he had difficulty remembering where the kitchen was she kindly informed him that he was fired. He thanked her gratefully and staggered away in Finn's wake.

Nick stood, swaying, in the middle of the kitchen watching Maggie get out the coffee beans. His air of puzzlement gave way to an anguished groan when she viciously held down the button on the electric grinder.

'You look awful,' she said, with some satisfaction. 'Sit down, why don't you, before you fall down?' She pushed a chair his way and he sat down suddenly, almost missing it.

Since she was so rarely in the kitchen it took her a while to find the essentials, and her fumbling wasn't helped by the knowledge that those dull slate eyes were following her every move. By the time she slapped his black coffee in front of him she was a bundle of exposed nerve-ends.

'Well, drink up,' she snapped, when he made no move to pick it up.

'I don't want any coffee.'

Maggie was infuriated. 'Then why did you sit there and let me go to the trouble of making it?'

He smiled in bemusement. His eyes, she realised, weren't so much dull as glazed. 'Nick, what *do* you want? You were the one who insisted on coming in. Nick?'

'What do I want?' He shook his head slowly from side to side. 'You *know* what I want, Maggie.'

'I wouldn't be asking if I did.'

His eyes took on an even more feverish glaze. 'You.'

'Me?' She stared at him, her heart beating erratically. He was drunk. He didn't know what he was saying. She shouldn't encourage him. It was totally wrong to try and get information out of him in this vulnerable state. Who knew what secrets he might let slip? Her heart beat even faster. 'You want me? Why?'

'Because,' he said expansively, waving his uninjured hand in expressive curves.

'Because why?' she breathed, moving closer and half bending. To the devil with right or wrong, she had to know...

'Because I...' He stopped and a flicker of dismay crossed his face. 'Because you're a witch, Maggie Cole,' he continued hazily. 'Because I think I'm...I'm...'

'You're what?' She forced her voice to remain soft and sweet and welcoming when she really felt like throttling him for his confusion. Was he going to say that he was falling in love with her? 'You can tell me, I won't give away your secret.'

'I'm...I'm...I'm going to lie down...'

He slid gracefully out of the chair on to the blue slate tiles of the kitchen floor.

Nick Fortune was out for the count.

CHAPTER NINE

MAGGIE swallowed to relieve the pressure in her ears and smiled at Thomas, snoring gently in the seat next to her. He had slept for almost the entire eleven hours of the flight from Los Angeles, exhausted by the thrills of Disneyland.

Maggie was finding the reverse to be true. The thrill of uncertainty that accompanied her newly single state had kept her awake through two bad movies and three indifferent meals. It felt as though she were carrying her own personal Disneyland around inside her—she was up one minute and down the next.

Patience not being one of her virtues, Maggie hadn't been able to wait until she got back to spring her surprise on Finn. Bursting with her own cleverness, she had called him from the judge's office as soon as the stiff little document that pronounced that their marriage no longer existed was in her hands.

At first she thought that Finn had fainted again. When he could speak he had been furious at her for her tasteless joke. It was only by putting Thomas on that he was convinced, and even then some of his shocked anger lingered. He should have been at least *consulted* on his opinion, he told her. He could have at least been *prepared*. But Maggie could detect the threads of relief that it was all over, and that the hideous burden of responsibility had been snatched away from him. A kind of crazy sadness and joy had zinged across the telephone line. It was the end of an era, of a great, glorious game they had both played with youthful enthusiasm. Now it was time to accept maturity.

Maggie didn't feel mature at this moment. She felt very young and uncertain. Truth and consequences—she had evaded them for so long that she had almost believed that the day of reckoning would never come. The publicity was going to be a pain, and Markham and Paddy were going to hit their respective ceilings, but somehow those twin threats had lost their power. It was Nick whom Maggie feared, and feared *for*. Nick who mattered. For all his wealth and power he was very much a loner, his daughter the only one with whom he shared any emotional closeness. Who would be there to help assuage his sense of loss, of rage and betrayal? To temper the hurt of what he must inevitably see as another rejection of his love? Maggie's heart ached for him...and for herself, for she was the last person he would turn to.

Five nights ago, when he had collapsed on her kitchen floor, it had taken all Maggie's strength to half drag, half carry him through to the lounge and ease him down on to the white leather couch in the conversation pit, taking care that his right arm didn't slide out of its sling. The couch was long but narrow, and Maggie had been worried that he might fall off if he tried to turn over in his sleep so she had wedged him in with cushions and firmly tucked a soft cashmere blanket around him after removing his shoes and socks. She had knelt beside him for a while, watching the slow, even rise and fall of the broad chest, studying the softened lines of the harsh face, openly admiring him in a way she wasn't allowed to when he was awake. When she reluctantly went back to bed she licensed herself to one gentle, lingering kiss on that sensual sleep-soft mouth. He had stirred and she had held her breath, but to her disappointment and relief he had settled again, a slight, dreamy smile indenting one stubbled cheek.

It seemed that she barely slept before she was awake again. It was light outside, but still early, much earlier than Maggie usually stirred, especially after a late night.

She rolled over and peered groggily at the blurred figure pulling back the curtains on the glorious view of the city and harbour. She winced as the warm summer light streaked across the bed. Even the heady aroma of coffee didn't mollify her.

'For goodness' sake, Sam, isn't this carrying remorse to ridiculous extremes?' she groaned, burying her face in the heap of pillows. 'Just consider yourself forgiven and let me go back to sleep.'

'Sam? Is he the man you usually wake up to, Maggie?'

Maggie shot upright in the bed, pushing the heavy black tangle of hair out of her eyes, clutching the bed-clothes to her chest.

'Nick! W-what are you doing here?'

'I thought it would be extremely ill-mannered of me to leave without thanking my hostess . . . especially after the tender loving care she offered me when I was at her mercy. I made coffee.' He put the cup down on her bedside table.

'In the kitchen? Sam hates anyone else messing around in his kitchen,' Maggie babbled. How much did he remember about last night?

'I won't tell if you won't. I doubt if either Sam or your husband will surface for a while, and when they do they'll have the devil of a hangover.'

Your husband. He never called Finn by his given name. It was as if he felt the need constantly to remind them both of her obligations.

'And you don't?' she countered, ignoring the coffee. She just wanted him to leave. He had removed his sling, and his grimy, tattered shirt. Stripped to the waist, he was a shock to the senses—and the imagination. He had displayed more bare flesh on the beach but here, in her pink and white bedroom, his half-nakedness was somehow more indecent, aggressively erotic. His hard muscles rippled and shifted across the deep chest with every breath he took. What would happen if he reached over and lifted her into his arms? Would she scream or sigh with pleasure?

'I wasn't that drunk.'

Maggie snorted in disbelief. 'You hardly even knew what you were saying. And you passed out on the floor.'

'That was the medication I had, not the booze. I certainly wasn't as tanked as your husband and his babysitter.'

His derogatory tone annoyed her.

'If you weren't drunk, why did you get into a fight?'

'Your husband wasn't taking no for an answer.'

'You could have just walked away, if you knew that he wasn't responsible for what he was saying.'

'I didn't say he wasn't responsible, I said he was drunk. And I'd had just enough to lower my resistance to insult. I lost my temper—but I never lost control. I can't afford to, because with my skill I could kill someone, so when I drink I always stay within my limit. I haven't been in a brawl since I became a professional fighter.'

'Oh, Finn *will* be flattered to know that you made an exception for him,' said Maggie sarcastically.

'Since he was the reason I was drinking in the first place, it seemed only fitting. I won't deny I enjoyed beating the hell out of him.'

'By the looks of things the honours were roughly even,' Maggie said tartly, looking at his strapped hand.

'I broke it on his jaw.' Nick's reminiscent smile contained a cruel satisfaction.

Maggie's shocked remonstrance fell prey to a delayed thought. 'What do you mean, he was the reason you were drinking? I thought...I mean, weren't you at the nightclub with someone?' That question had haunted the edges of her sleep.

'You mean a date?' Unexpectedly he sat down on the edge of the bed, and Maggie had to scrabble up the slope to stay away from him, to keep herself from reaching out to touch that warm, glossy skin. Her wide eyes remained fixed on him as his mouth twisted ironically. 'No, I wasn't with another woman. I'm a monogamist, Maggie, I've only ever wanted one woman at a time. And this time the woman I want is already spoken for. So when I came face to face with the speaker—who happened to be spoiling for a fight—why shouldn't I have accepted the chance to work off my frustrations? I may have won the battle, but he still controls the war. He still has you.'

Maggie swallowed, her eyes sliding away from the darkened desire in his. 'But...Finn said you were fighting over Laurie.'

'We were. After all, he doesn't know about you and me, does he? I hit him once for Laurie...but all the other times were for you.'

Maggie was appalled. 'You could have killed him.'

Again that ironic smile. 'That would have solved my problem, wouldn't it? But no, I know my own strength. I swore when I left the ring that I'd never use my fists again. You make me want to do a lot of things I'd sworn never to do, Maggie...' His injured fist touched her chin, and her hand came up to push it away but somehow it became entwined with his. Nick looked down at their joining, and Maggie realised that it was her scarred hand that had reached out. Nick had already seen the worst of her. With him there was none of her usual self-consciousness.

'We're quite a pair, aren't we?' he murmured.

She shook her head, not knowing what to say without blurting out her feelings. 'You shouldn't be here.'

'In your bedroom? On your bed? It is yours, isn't it, Maggie? You and your husband have separate rooms, and separate dressing-rooms and bathrooms. There's not one sign of a crossover, not a stray sock or brush. Even the connecting door between you is locked.'

'You've been snooping!' Maggie accused, snatching her hand away.

'I was intrigued about your domestic arrangements.' He shrugged, a marvellous exercise in musculature.

'Finn and I respect each other's privacy, which is obviously more than you do. Will you please get off the bed?'

'What do you do when you want a bit of togetherness? Slip an engraved invitation under the door?'

'None of your business. Don't you have an office or something to go to?'

'Today's Sunday,' he pointed out. 'I can't believe that a passionate, sensuous woman like you can be happy with this kind of sterile arrangement.'

'I . . . I'm a light sleeper and Finn snores,' Maggie invented desperately.

'You don't think the sheets have anything to do with it . . . your disturbed sleep patterns, I mean?'

'What do you mean?' said Maggie blankly, grappling to keep up with him.

'The colour. Isn't it a bit . . . er . . . *violent* for your colour scheme? Everything else is so beautifully co-ordinated . . .'

Maggie had forgotten all about them. Now her complexion almost matched. The only thing to do was brazen it out.

'These old things?' she said, looking straight into his amused eyes. 'I've had them for years.'

He studied the unfaded red silk with raised eyebrows. 'I'm too much of a gentleman to call you a liar.'

'You just did! If you're not going to leave the least you can do is put your shirt on,' she said, hoping to get both their minds off her sleeping arrangements.

'It's in a disgusting state. Think of the speculation it would cause if I was seen leaving your apartment looking as though I'd had my clothes ripped off. I thought you might find me something suitable . . .'

'I doubt if you'd fit into anything of mine,' Maggie said, perversely acting obtuse when she should be leaping at the chance to hustle him away.

'Oh, I don't know.' His eyes roamed over the primly tucked sheet. 'As I recall, you're fairly well built——'

'Finn's things would be too small for you,' she said hurriedly. 'I'll have to get something from Sam. I suggest you wait downstairs. I can do without another fight on my hands.'

'I think last night got it out of my system,' he said, not moving. 'Now, if only I could get *you* out of my system I'd be my own man again...' He shifted an arm across the other side of her body and leaned closer, forcing her back against the heaped pillows. She put her hands flat against his bare chest, which was a mistake. She could feel his heartbeat, the tiny electrical thrills that rippled just under his skin, communicating the desire that was echoed in his darkening eyes. Her hands moved compulsively, grazing his hard nipples in a way that made his body shake on a wordless moan. He filled her vision and her senses; her whole being was focused on the slow, erotic approach of that lush and languorous mouth. Her expression told him everything.

'*Maggie!*' The harsh explosion jerked her back to reality. Finn, wearing a rich brocade robe and looking distinctly the worse for wear, was hanging in shock from the handle of the open bedroom door. 'What in the hell is going on here?'

Nick resisted the frantic push from Maggie's hands which, a moment before, had been sliding luxuriantly into the thick dark hair at the back of his head. He took his time sitting back, but even then he didn't remove his entrapping arm. Maggie peeped over it at her shocked husband, wishing that, chameleon-like, her blush could hide her among her wicked sheets.

'What does it look like?' Nick ground o challengingly.

'Maggie?' Finn's stunned gaze moved from one to the other.

'I had to let him stay, Finn,' Maggie protested weakly, 'I couldn't very well tell him to leave when he was unconscious. And you and Sam were no help—you were dead to the world as well! What should I have done? Phoned Laurie, and dragged her out in the middle of the night?'

'No, of course not,' Finn stammered, unwilling to leave the support of the door, his face as pale as his sling. 'But surely you didn't have to *sleep* with him?'

'I didn't!' Maggie struggled to sit up, only to find herself pushed back. 'For goodness' sake, Finn, use your brain. If you have any brain cells *left* after last night!'

Her voice rose, and Finn leaned his head against the door. 'All right, Maggie, keep your hair on. I'm sorry, but when I came in and saw him like that...' He shrugged apologetically, and winced at what the gesture did to his fragile constitution.

Maggie didn't dare look at Nick, but she could feel the tension emanating from the powerful body.

'You mean, you actually believe her?' The gravelly accent gave her a clue to Nick's intention. He was playing the raw, self-made man to Finn's languid aristocrat. Maggie had to admit that in that ornate robe, his handsome face pale and wan, his hangover draining his energy, Finn did rather look the part. Never had the differences between the two men been so marked. Finn had his strengths, but his superficial beauty tended to obscure them, whereas one only had to look at Nick to know that he was a rock that one could shelter beside, or dash oneself to pieces against. What Nick's ruggedness obscured was his passion, his sensitivity.

'Of course I believe her.' Finn arched his brows in a fine expression of haughty distaste which was offset by the peevish edge to his words. He, too, realised he was being taunted.

'You find a man and your wife half naked in her bed and you swallow her claim that it's perfectly innocent?'

'Of course. Maggie would never lie to me,' responded Finn evenly, but he flicked a glance at Maggie, and she remembered her lie of omission about her trip to America. Her eyes evaded Finn's. 'She never has before,' he added firmly, making her feel more guilty than ever.

'There's always a first time,' said Nick cynically, his remark containing the harsh echoes of past experience.

'I know Maggie. And I know that she'd never indulge in casual sex with a stranger, let alone *you*.' Finn clipped off the last word, regretting the slip.

'But Maggie and I aren't strangers,' Nick's uninjured hand moved to stroke the black curls spread out on the pillow, weaving them around his fingers, not taking his eyes off the man in the doorway. 'We're better acquainted than you imagine, aren't we, honey?'

'Nick . . .' Her protest died. It was useless appealing to that aggressive profile. He intended to complete verbally what he had begun physically last night . . . the vanquishment of a very personal enemy. 'Finn . . . you look terrible, why don't you get back to bed? I'll explain everything later, when we're *alone* . . .'

'Anxious to get rid of you, isn't she?' suggested Nick with a guttural softness that overrode the warning in her words. Still without taking his eyes off Finn, his hand left her hair to rest over the scarred hand nervously crumpling the sheet. Finn stiffened at the casual familiarity with a flaw that was Maggie's second best-kept secret.

'Maggie——'

'He's winding you up, Finn. Of *course* I haven't slept with him,' she said desperately. 'I know what's at stake, you know I wouldn't jeopardise that! He's only making insinuations to annoy you—you know it's not the truth.'

'Perhaps not the literal truth. But ask her, Cole, if she would *like* it to be the truth. Ask your wife if she loves *you* the way a woman should love a man. Then ask her how she feels about *me*!'

With such devastating arrogance and accuracy he laid Maggie's heart and soul bare.

'Nick...' Her voice was a whisper of pain. He knew. He had made her love him for precisely this reason. To use against Finn.

'Legally she's yours, Cole...but in every way that matters she's *mine*!' He cut off Finn's muffled sound of shock. 'Oh, she might still mouth expressions of love and loyalty towards you, but that's all they are...the empty words of habit, the fond remembrances of childhood. As a boy you might have satisfied Maggie's need for companionship, but as a man you can't cut it. If she had any real physical or emotional love for the man you are she wouldn't respond to me the way she does...like a woman starving to be loved, a woman seeking to be desired, touched...'

Maggie closed her eyes to the humiliation. He made her sound like a sex-crazed waif, begging for the crumbs of his affection. Oh, God, had she been so brazenly obvious...?

'And you think you're the man to do that?' Finn sneered, but there was an odd note to his voice that made Maggie peep through her lashes. Finn's face was smooth and bland. It was his 'negotiating face'.

'The point is that you're *not*. And when Maggie admits that to herself she'll leave you. Just as my daughter will find you less than attractive without your glamorous trappings of wealth and status——'

'I think you do Laurie an injustice——'

'It's your choice, Cole. You can have Laurie, or you can have everything else—your company, your flashy lifestyle, your privileged status...' Nick's mocking ultimatum offered no compromise.

'And Maggie...do I get to keep Maggie, too, if I give up Laurie?' Finn asked coolly.

'Would you want to keep her, knowing that she's in love with *me*?' taunted Nick with triumphant savagery.

It was too much for Maggie, who suddenly exploded out of the bed. How casual he was about announcing her love, as if it were something he had just picked up in the street on the offchance it would be useful, rather than a unique gift to be honoured and cherished.

'Get out, both of you!' she screeched, putting the length of the room between them. 'Get out of my room! In fact, get out of my *life*!' She picked up a shoe.

'Maggie, calm down, I was only trying to get him to——' Finn ducked as a shoe struck the door-frame mere centimetres from his head. It was followed by another. Maggie had plenty of ammunition.

'Maggie——'

'Shut up! Shut up! Shut up!' Three shoes in perfect rhythm as Finn backed into the safety of the hallway. 'I'm sick of you trying to tell me that everything's going to be all right. It's *not*! Just go away and leave me alone!'

Finn knew from experience that it was wise advice. Nick was not so privileged. His stunned expression was replaced by one that raked Maggie raw.

'I think you just made your choice, Maggie.' His exultant words confirmed his smug assumption of victory. He came towards her, unafraid, smiling, gloating, full of the pride of possession. Oh, yes, he wanted her *now* . . . but what would happen later if she gave in? Her love would still be with her, but his pride would turn to hatred, his desire to contempt. And she would be left with *nothing*. Less than nothing, for she would have the full knowledge of what she had lost.

'Yes, and I choose neither of you!' she hissed, rearming herself.

He kept coming and she threw wildly, but it was the desperation in her voice rather than the shoes which found their mark which stopped him. 'You were just a bit of fun, Nick, but now the party's over and it's time to go home.'

'Nice try, Maggie,' he told her evenly. 'But I'm not as trusting as your husband. Or as easy to get rid of...'

But she did get rid of him, in the end. Not because of the frantic lies she flung at his hard head, but because she finally locked herself in the bathroom and refused to come out. The ultimate cop-out, and he knew it.

'I'll be back, Maggie,' he threatened through the door's protection. 'Don't think that this is the end of it. You may hate what you feel for me but you can't escape it. I won't let you. You can run, you can hide, you can pretend to be the callous, haughty bitch I know you're not, but you can't escape me. Do you hear me, Maggie? I'm coming back for you if I have to walk through the wall to get you!'

Famous last words. She *had* escaped...to America, land of the free!

Maggie woke Thomas as the plane steepened its descent and tried to fill her mind with the trivialities of travel rather than the tribulations of a beleaguered heart. As first-class passengers they were through Customs and Immigration quickly, and the widowed Thomas was met by his daughter and two grandchildren, who squealed with delight over the Disney souvenirs he had brought them. Maggie waved them off from the concourse and then looked around for Sam. There was no sign of him, and she was just debating whether to slip back into the terminal to exchange her remaining US dollars for New Zealand currency when a car screeched up to the kerb beside her luggage. Her cases were off the luggage trolley and in the car boot before Maggie recovered from her thrill of horror.

'How dare you? You can't do that! Take them out!'

Nick shoved her into the car with all the repressed violence with which he had handled the bags.

'Honey, the mood I'm in I can do what the hell I like!'

Maggie believed him. They shot out of the temporary parking area with such rapidity that she was thrust back in her seat. Several vicious gear-changes later her stomach stablised sufficiently for her to murmur, 'Sam was going to pick me up. He's going to wonder where I am.'

'You mean you don't make a habit of disappearing whenever you feel like it?' he growled tightly.

'I . . . I didn't disappear.'

'As far as *I* was concerned you did. I told you I'd be back. Did you think I didn't mean it?'

'I . . .' Did he know? Had Laurie broken the news? Is that what had put him in this ugly mood? Maggie licked her lips and tried a gentle probe. 'I wasn't sure . . . but I had to go—it was all arranged.'

'Who by? The ageing Romeo?' he grated, weaving in and out of traffic with reckless ease.

Maggie stared at him blankly, then she remembered the farewell-and-thank-you kiss she had given Thomas. 'That was my lawyer.'

His eyebrows shot up as he braked abruptly at a red light. 'You take your lawyer on holiday with you? Though that shouldn't really surprise me. You have a talent for creating trouble—you probably need a lawyer the way other women need a maid.'

'I am not a troublemaker!'

'You've certainly made enough for me. In the short time we've known each other you've caused me no end of problems. I do *not* appreciate having doors slammed in my face as if I were some stray dog begging for a bone.'

Maggie quailed. 'I only went into the bathroom because I was tired of being hectored——'

'I wasn't talking about that. I was talking about the last few days. Neither your husband nor that Man Friday of yours told me you were away. As far as I was concerned, you were holed up in that apartment like a snivelling coward——'

'I am *not* a coward!' Her temper flared, burning off her fear.

'No? Then why did you run away?'

'I wasn't running *away*, I was running *to*——' Her moment of revelation was ruined by the blare of a horn. The light was green, and probably had been for some time. Nick swivelled round in his seat and punched a savage look at the impatient driver behind them, who responded with a crude gesture. For a moment Maggie thought Nick was going to get out of the car and exact retribution. He was definitely at boiling-point. To her relief he merely contented himself with a descriptive curse, rammed the car into gear and took off.

'Nick...? Nick, this isn't the way to the apartment—where are we going? Nick, aren't you going a little bit fast——'

'Don't tell me how to drive, Maggie. I might be tempted to stop the car and show you exactly how *you* drive *me*.'

Maggie wasn't sure whether it was a promise or a threat; it had dark elements of both. She decided discretion was the better part of valour, and even restrained herself from saying, 'I told you so' when they were pulled over by a young traffic officer who was righteously scathing about the antics of reckless drivers in fast, expensive cars, particularly drivers who were handicapped by bandaged hands.

Nick was sullen and monosyllabic in his replies as he produced his licence, and not all Maggie's apologetic charm could reduce the impact of his surly impatience with authority. She could have said that Nick one-handed could do more than most men could with *both* hands, but she didn't like to antagonise the officer more than Nick had already. The ticket was laboriously written and passed over, along with another little homily that was received in stony-faced silence.

It was not much further on that Nick, now driving with aggravatingly exaggerated care, swung off into the forecourt of a large, imposing house hidden behind a high brick wall. Maggie recognised the distinctive style of a leading avant-garde architect; brick and cedar and glass, arranged in deceptively simple lines which concealed the complex beauty within. Rather like the house's owner, Maggie thought nervously, knowing now where he had brought her.

'Nick, I don't think ...'

He opened her door for her. 'Good. Because I'm not giving you a choice. I'm through giving you choices, Maggie. Get out.'

She didn't get a chance to satisfy her curiosity about the interior of the house. It was all just a blur as she was hauled up a series of platforms and ramps until she found herself standing in what was obviously a very masculine master bedroom.

Nick immediately began stripping off his jacket and tie, cursing at the ineptness of his injured hand.

Maggie cleared her throat. 'How are your fingers?'

'I'll live,' he said tersely, attacking the buttons of his shirt.

'W-what are you doing?'

'Proving something to you.' That he was a man? He had already done that, many times over, but Maggie was riveted by the fumbling striptease.

'I don't understand ... Laurie ... ?' She was floundering around in the dark, afraid to say too much.

'Is out. And the staff don't come, uninvited, into my bedroom. No one does. This time we don't have to worry about interruptions. You know, don't you, that if your husband hadn't walked in on us we might already have been lovers by now ...'

'No ... Nick ...' She took several steps back. *Your husband.* He still didn't know—he didn't know any of it. 'We have to talk ... I have to tell you——'

He shook his head, ripping open another button, moving in on her. 'No. I understand perfectly. You're confused, uncertain, afraid to trust yourself or me. Given your past experience, and the things I've said to you about my feelings on marriage, it's not surprising that you ran away. But you don't have to be afraid of loving me, Maggie, not any more. I'm going to prove to you that you're more important to me than principles or pride. I want us to be lovers. I want you to feel secure and well-loved when you ask your husband for a divorce... I want you to feel committed, to *me*. I want you to know the pleasure that you'll be missing if you let loyalty to that ungrateful bastard overcome your love for me. We belong together, Maggie. I still believe in the vows of marriage, but Cole was a bitter mistake for you, and no one should have to endure a lifetime's imprisonment for a youthful folly. I...' His fluid intensity stumbled and Maggie felt her heart leave her chest. His cherished beliefs, his self-imposed rules for living, he was scattering them to the winds just for *her*.

He pulled off his shirt and reached for her. 'I love you, Maggie. I want to marry you. We belong to each other. I can't fight that any more. I don't care if you're another man's wife——' he groaned as he found her mouth '—as long as you love me, I can bear anything. Say it, Maggie. Tell me I'm not wrong...'

'No...'

He misunderstood her denial. His head wrenched back, his eyes burning with anguish. If Maggie had doubted the passion of his words and his body, she couldn't doubt his fear. Nick Fortune was hers.

'No, you're not wrong. I love you, Nick, more than I knew it was possible to love anyone——' She was buried in his kiss.

The smart little black leather gloves she wore slid across his bunched shoulders as his mouth thrust her back with the force of his hunger. Her touch was like a match to gasoline fumes. His body surged, his heavy thigh pushed between her legs, riding up the short skirt of her black and white polka-dot suit, a summery piece of nothing that enabled her to feel every ridge and muscle of him. But even in the tempestuous grip of blind passion, Maggie knew that she owed him the right to his principles. They were important to him, an integral part of his character. He needed to know that she respected them, too.

'Nick . . . he's not my husband . . .'

'Who?' His hands were on her thighs under the thin skirt, the tape on his fingers a rough contrast to his silken touch.

'Finn. We're not married any more. That's why I went to America with Thomas. I . . . I have the papers in my bag.' It had dropped unnoticed to the floor in the first moment of their embrace. Nick's mouth froze on her throat. He peeled himself back, slowly.

'You're divorced?' he asked hoarsely.

Semantics didn't seem to matter right now. Maggie nodded, searching his stunned eyes. 'We were never really married. You see, Finn and I——'

He didn't let her finish. The knowledge that she was now utterly his robbed him of the last atom of his control . . . and she was his willing partner in crime.

Her first time wasn't quite what Maggie had imagined it would be. There was no long, leisurely foreplay, no gentle awakening to the power and pleasure of being a woman, none of the pain that she had expected at the first invasion of her body. There was nothing but the rush and roar of blood in her veins, the overpowering feel and taste of male desire, a hungry urgency that built and built and built until the glorious sensation of fullness and tightness exploded in exquisite release as her lover shook and groaned and convulsed in his own, magnificent, thrusting climax. Afterwards they were both weak with the shock of it.

'I'm sorry,' he whispered, a trembling hand stroking her damp brow. 'Did I hurt you? I couldn't stop myself. The taste of you was like a shot of whisky to an alcoholic.' He began to ease his crushing weight from her.

'No...don't leave me!' she cried, wrapping her arms around his slick, muscled torso.

'I'll never do that,' he promised, kissing a tiny reddened mark on her breast, nuzzling the velvety underside of the creamy mound. Out of the corner of his eye he caught sight of the scattering of clothes on the floor around them, and grinned ruefully.

'This isn't what I intended. I had meant to court you with soft kisses and woo you to my bed. Instead I tear off your clothes like a maniac and take you on the floor.'

'You weren't taking, I was giving,' Maggie told him.

'I noticed,' he said huskily, and her eyes widened as she felt him, still softly locked inside her, thicken and stir. The thrills of excitement which had died away to a pleasant ache began to ripple through her body again. She was shocked when he suddenly withdrew, and he laughed at her dismay.

'No, not again. This time we do it properly,' he told her, lifting her easily and placing her on the wide bed where she pouted at him, delighting in her new-found confidence. She could make this big, powerful man shake like a kitten for the stroke of her hand.

'White sheets? What a disappointment,' she teased, running her hand over the crisp linen that was smooth under the wine-coloured duvet.

'Not with you on them.' He joined her, enjoying her frank and fascinated appraisal of his virility. 'That's not my only fantasy about you. I have others. And we have time to explore them all.' He cupped her breast possessively. 'I only wish I had full use of my other hand. Some of my fantasies call for a little more finesse than I possess right now.'

'You mean...there's more?' popped out before she could help it, and she blushed. He hadn't said anything about her virginity, but he had apologised for the fierceness with which he had possessed her. The knowledge of her inexperience embarrassed her. He was being delicate, not bombarding her with questions about it, and she loved him anew for his sensitivity. Her eyes, shyly evading his, fell on her hands.

'My gloves! I forgot to take them off!'

He gave her an odd look and picked up her left hand, halting her flustered movement. 'I liked it...the feel of leather against my skin, stroking me, holding me...'

Her flush deepened. Or perhaps it was that he had shrunk from the alternative—that ugly mass of scars. As if he could read her mind, Nick took off her glove, ignoring her half-hearted attempt to stop him. With his bandaged hand he made her look at him, and then he began to stroke her skin very lightly with the fingertips of the glove. He traced a pattern from collarbone to hip, trailing teasing circles around her breasts until they became unbearably swollen, and covering every inch of her quivering belly and soft thighs to culminate at last with a featherlight touch whispering against the living jewel he had so coveted. Maggie gasped, her body arching helplessly.

'You like it, too,' he told her, darkened eyes haunting hers. 'You like everything I do to you. Don't be shy with me, Maggie, don't hold back, don't ever hold anything back.' The glove began to move again, but more firmly, more explicitly, stroking and exciting her until she exploded in his arms and he swept her against him, holding her hard until she had finished shaking, and then taking her poor, scarred hand and cupping it around the proof of his desire. 'I need to know everything, every desire, every fear...so that I can share them, too. You could never disgust me. I love you just the way you are...'

She realised that he had thought that she had left her gloves on deliberately and had sought to reassure her in the most graphic way possible. She could have wept at the depth of love and sensitivity he had shown, but instead she returned his gift with interest, becoming a wicked wanton without inhibition, casting out all her doubts in the physical expression of her joy.

The day drew blissfully on, the bright morning shading into golden afternoon and mellow evening. Their dialogue was largely silent, words weren't necessary and the rest of the world had ceased to exist. The phone rang and they ignored it. They made love, showered, made love again and slept only to wake again eager to partake of another feast of passion.

It was almost sunset before they emerged from their mutual absorption. They were lying, sweetly entangled in the no longer virgin sheets when the phone beside the bed rang again, and with a groan Nick reached out a languid arm to answer it.

At least it sounded like a telephone. How was Maggie to know that it was a bell tolling the death-knell of a perfect day?

On the other end of the line was an operative from a private detection agency. And while Maggie cuddled dreamily against the hard curve of his back, Nick Fortune learned that his daughter had just eloped with his lover's ex-husband.

CHAPTER TEN

MAGGIE stared at the alien sight on her plate. Bacon and eggs and hash-brown potatoes. Her forbidden favourites.

'What's this?' she asked in horror.

'Food,' Sam told her. 'Remember? That stuff we eat to keep us alive—if we want to live, that is. You said you hadn't eaten since the flight. That's over thirty-six hours.'

As a cure for her misery it was a disaster. Maggie took another look at the tempting spread under her nose, clapped a hand to her mouth, and ran to the bathroom.

'This doesn't mean what I think it means, does it?' asked Sam cautiously, offering her a cup of his special cure-all coffee when she returned.

'No, I am not pregnant,' said Maggie flatly. Even that first, frantic time Nick had taken a moment to protect her... or was it himself? Who knew what one could pick up from a promiscuous tart! He hadn't known... even afterwards, he hadn't known! What kind of insensitive creep didn't know a virgin when he had one?

'Just asking,' said Sam, looking down at her slumped figure with concern. 'Are you going to tell me, or am I going to have to keep guessing?'

'Why, Sam? Why did they go off like that without telling me?' she asked wearily, answering his question with one of her own. 'Do you think it was because they knew about the detective? But then they must have known that as soon as they applied for a marriage licence the cat would be well and truly out of the bag! And how did they get one, anyway? Laurie is still under age!'

Sam coughed. 'It was all very spur of the moment and, actually, I think it was all Laurie's idea. She got the licence. I think she felt ... well, we all realised that there was something going on between you and Fortune ... I think she sort of wanted to repay you for all your unselfishness by trying to clear the decks for you ..'

Maggie groaned. 'I think throwing the baby out with the bathwater is a better phrase.'

'Do you love him, Maggie? Is he in love with you?'

'Oh, God, I don't know,' she said drearily. 'Everything is such a mess. How *could* he love me, after what I did? And when he finds out that Laurie is pregnant——!' She felt the shattering of her dreams all over again. The tears that she had ached to cry all night, and couldn't, suddenly burst forth and she fell sobbing into Sam's strong care.

She had seen Nick in a rage, but nothing had prepared her for the man of stone he had become after that damning phone-call. He had been utterly emotionless as he had informed her of the detective's findings. Then he had asked a single question. Had she got her 'quickie' divorce for her own sake, or because she knew that Finn wanted to marry Laurie?

It was too simple a question for her to answer quickly and her hesitation condemned her.

'And was this little dalliance part of the plan too? Were you supposed to keep me occupied in bed while they made their getaway? How delighted you must have been that I played so neatly into your hands.' The eyes that had been lit with warm highlights were glittering slivers of grey steel.

'No, Nick ... believe me, I had no idea that they were going to do this. They wanted a proper wedding——'

Her protest only made things worse. 'You mean you thought that you had a bit longer to wind me around your little finger? Did you think that I would be so weak with love that I'd forgive you *anything*? My God, and to think I was so close to sacrificing everything to this madness!' The sharp borders of his bloodless articulation showed how utterly he had banished the madness. The real Nick Fortune, the man, the lover, was back behind the polished steel barriers of bitter experience. He was pulling on his clothes, and with every item of clothing he removed himself further from the passionate lover to whom Maggie had given her heart.

'Nick, please, you must listen——'

'Why? So that you can give them more time?'

'But—what are you going to do?'

'Go after them.'

'But—do you know where they are?'

'No. But I'll find them,' he said grimly, with certainty, and Maggie was reminded of his ruthless single-mindedness. He had wanted her, hadn't he? And now he had had her he was free to turn his mind to something else. 'I don't suppose it would do any good to ask you to tell me where they are.'

'No.' In this she knew less than he, but he didn't give her time to tell him that.

'I thought not. Get dressed.' He threw her her skirt and jacket, impatient to be gone.

'Nick, please——'

He looked at her, the wild gypsy whom he had loved so thoroughly and so well, with complete indifference. 'You've had your fun. It's over.'

'Nick, I love you,' she begged desperately. 'You said you loved me.'

His smile was as chilled and bloodless as his lack of accent. 'Maybe I was being no more honest than you. I know which lies bring a woman most eagerly to bed...'

Maggie couldn't let him get away with it. 'I've never loved anyone the way that I love you——'

'Is that a compliment? Should the fly be flattered to be invited into the web? Were none of the others fool enough to trample on their self-respect for the sake of a——?'

He used a brutal phrase that made Maggie flinch. 'It was more than that, you know it was, Nick.' She stopped, thunderstruck. 'Others? W-what others?'

'Can't even be honest now, can you, Maggie?' he said with sickened contempt. 'You have a good body, but you use it rather too greedily and too well to pretend that you've not had a good many teachers.'

And while Maggie was struggling with the devastating realisation that he hadn't, after all, been apologising for taking her virginity so roughly, Nick picked up the phone, punched in a number and had a murmured conversation which she was too distraught to hear. There had been no actual *physical* evidence, certainly, to mourn the passing of her innocence, but surely men could tell when they were the first? Wasn't it part of the male instinct? How could man through the ages come to set virginity as such a prize if he couldn't recognise the winning of it? Maggie felt helpless . . . cheated out of a precious part of her womanhood, something she hadn't really appreciated the value of, until it was gone forever. She felt hurt, angry at Nick for his ignorance, for his quickness to condemn. He made her sexual awakening seem like the soiled lust of a hardened nymphomaniac. And all because he wanted to preserve his pride!

He put the phone down. 'Put your clothes on. Unless you'd rather be thrown out naked into the street. Perhaps that's a kick you haven't tried yet.'

She obeyed, but only because she couldn't argue in the nude while he was fully dressed. She was starting to button her jacket-blouse, searching for the words to reach him, when there was a brief tattoo on the door. Without even looking to see whether she was decently covered, Nick called out and a man walked in. He was thin and austere, dressed in a dark suit, circumspect of dress and demeanour even when he saw Maggie's shocked embarrassment.

'Yes, sir?'

'Escort Mrs Cole out. And, Jenson...'

'Yes, sir?'

'She is not to be readmitted. Under *any* circumstances.'

'Understood, sir.' Jenson's face didn't change, so perhaps Maggie imagined his contempt.

'Nick, you can't do this——'

'Watch me.'

'At least let me call for a taxi——' Hating to beg, but anything to delay going, any opportunity to get him to listen...

'I think not.' He probably suspected that she wanted to call the runaways, to warn them...

'Nick, please——' She struggled to preserve what little dignity the presence of the other man left her.

'Oh? You want something for your trouble?' He walked over to the discreet bureau and picked up something from its polished surface. He tossed her a black velvet jeweller's box which she caught automatically. 'Enjoy your *baubles*, my dear. You earned them very prettily.'

He was making her sound like a common prostitute. She accepted at last that he was beyond reason or persuasion. His contempt was even beyond anger. He was sick to his soul at the very sight of her, intent on deliberately destroying whatever vestige of feeling there was left between them. That he was doing it in front of an audience told Maggie that from now on she could expect no mercy from him. Her worst-case scenario had come true. There was nothing left to salvage.

'I need my bag.' She had forgotten her gloves, too, but in the state she was in she didn't notice. Nick did, but he stilled his infinitesimal movement towards her with ruthless swiftness. No more. He would kill her before he showed her a moment's compassion. Her hand was a symbol of what she was: a flawed masterpiece, a

worthless treasure. The knowledge was bitter gall. He
was twice a fool.

With her back to the two men Maggie picked up her
handbag from the bedside table and opened it. There
were too many lies between them but this one she could
put to rest. She couldn't hand him the envelope containing her annulment papers. In his present mood he
would probably tear it up without even opening it. She
would leave it and hope that he would open it later out
of curiosity. He could scarcely dismiss the affidavit of
one of Auckland's leading gynaecologists as a lie! She
laid the envelope quietly to rest beside the telephone.
Lifting her chin, she turned and walked across the room.
When she reached Nick she paused.

'Goodbye, Nick.'

Her quiet dignity reached him as her wild protests had
not. His eyes flickered away to the rumpled bed, tes-
timony to their long, lazy day of loving, and hardened
there.

'You've forgotten your jewellery, Maggie. You ought
to walk away with something of value from this fiasco,
don't you think? Other than ...experience.'

The poison-tipped lash caressed them both with its
bitter sting. 'I've forgotten nothing,' she told him
steadily, her pride and all her love flashing in her eyes.
'And nor have you. I hope you never will.'

She meant the fact that he had loved her. No matter
how furiously he denied it now, for a few brief hours
she had known the fullness of his love. He could never
take that away from her, never make her regret it, no
matter what the future brought.

'Oh, Sam ...' she whispered now, trying to wipe away
weak tears at the memory of her last glimpse of Nick,
grey-faced, his eyes buring with a queer, cold rage. As
soon as she had got back to the apartment, before she
had fallen apart at the seams, she had tried to get in
touch with Finn at the Rotorua hotel at which Sam said

he and Laurie were staying. But there had been no reply from the room, although the clerk said they had checked in. So, on top of her sleepless agony over the ignominious end to the first and only love-affair of her life, there had been added the worry of what Nick would do when he caught up with his daughter.

'What are we going to do? What am *I* going to do?' She meant with the rest of her life, a life without Nick's wonderful, infuriating presence.

Sam chose to misunderstand her. 'Wait. That's all we can do. Look at it this way. If *we* can't find them, neither can *he*. Maybe they checked out of that hotel because they figured they were too easy to trace there. Maybe our phone-calls spooked them.'

In her blind misery Maggie didn't respond to the challenge. She was fresh out of clever ideas. They were what had got her into this mess.

'Maggie...' Sam knelt by her chair and pulled her head on to his broad shoulder. 'It's not your fault they fell in love, so don't take the blame for it. If he's worthy of your love, he'll forgive you the lies, especially when he sees how happy Laurie is, how right those two are for each other...'

Maggie's head rolled in sodden protest. 'He's never going to forgive me. Never! You didn't see his face! Even if he still loves me, his damned pride won't let him.' She gave a small hiccuping sob that was drowned out by the telephone on the wall. They both froze, then Sam leapt across to pick it up on the second ring.

'It's him!' he hissed, holding the receiver hard against his T-shirt. Maggie was a mere blur.

'Nick?' Her voice was tremulous with hope.

'Auckland Hospital. Accident and Emergency.' His voice was thick and harshly accusing. 'Your husband—your *ex-husband*—crashed his car.'

'Oh, my God! Are they——? How are they?'

'I don't know. I just got a call from the police. Laurie was conscious, but that was all they'd tell me.'

'And ... Finn?'

'I didn't ask.' And cared less was the implication. 'Be outside in five minutes. I'll take you.'

Sam went down with her and walked up and down the kerb in the light mist of rain under prophetically grey skies, listening patiently to her babble.

'He didn't have to offer me a lift. He could have left it to the police to call me. He must be out of his mind with worry but he took time to call me. He could get there a lot more quickly if he just drove through the park to the hospital but he's coming all out of his way just to get me ...'

The rain was warm but her teeth were chattering by the time the dark blue Jaguar that had abducted her from the airport drew up. Nick didn't bother getting out of the car. He leaned over and thrust open the passenger door, making a savage sound of impatience as Maggie hung back, suddenly afraid. Sam's hands steadied her as he pushed her forward.

'Look after her,' he told the white-knuckled driver. 'I'll follow in a while. I'll have to call Finn's grandfather.'

Nick nodded once, sharply, as if he didn't trust himself to speak. Maggie didn't trust herself either, but as the car slid through the shiny streets she had to ask, in a cracked whisper, 'Where were they? How did it happen?'

After a tortured silence, during which she thought he was going to ignore her, he said tersely, 'Coming down this side of the Bombay Hills.' This side? That meant that they were travelling back towards Auckland! 'There was an eight-car pile-up. A hell of a mess. They had to call in a helicopter to transport the seriously injured.'

There was another question that had to be asked. 'W— was it Finn's fault?'

'Yes, it was his fault,' snarled Nick, his words engorged with loathing. 'If he hadn't taken Laurie away

she wouldn't be there now...lying broken in some
damned hospital bed——'

The image was a hideous one. Now was no time to
point out that Laurie had been a willing participant in
the flight. Maggie must have made some small sound of
distress as she clenched her hands in her lap because Nick
took a savage, controlling breath.

'No, it wasn't his fault. He was in the wrong place at
the wrong time. Some other damned fool driving too
fast in the slick conditions crossed the centre strip.'

Maggie put a hand to her mouth, biting the lace of
the gloves she had pulled blindly on with the rest of her
clothes. She knew the kind of damage head-on motorway
smashes could wreak on the human body. Oh, God, what
if Finn...or Laurie...

Nick parked the car illegally outside the hospital and
Maggie had to run to keep up with him as he shoved
through the double doors of the emergency room. The
nurse on the reception desk took in their ragged air of
panic in one experienced glance, and very firmly took
the initiative, having accurately gauged Nick as a man
who wouldn't hesitate to throw his weight around if he
didn't get some answers—fast. She directed Maggie
through to X-ray, where they had taken Finn, and led
Nick out through another set of doors, where the doctors
were still working with Laurie.

Maggie nearly collapsed herself when she found Finn,
arguing weakly with the X-ray attendant, but apparently
in full possession of all his limbs and most of his
faculties.

'They're doing a skull X-ray—I was knocked out.' He
grabbed at Maggie gratefully. His shirt front was covered
with blood, but the cut above his eye wasn't deep, just
long. The bruised lump, though, was ominous. 'How's
Laurie? Have you seen her? Nobody knows...or they
won't tell me. Is Fortune here? Does he know? Tell him

to get some answers—find out what they're hiding. Maggie *please*, I have to know——'

'If you could calm him down I'd appreciate it,' the attendant said quietly to Maggie. 'He's been like a wild man, but we can't give him a sedative because of the possibility of concussion.'

'OK, Finn. I'll go and find out,' Maggie said, pressing him back on to the trolley.

'And you'll come straight back? Promise?'

'Of course I do. Lie down, Finn, I'll be back as soon as I can.'

People were beginning to trickle into the waiting-room, which had been virtually empty when they had arrived, but there was no sign of Nick. Maggie was debating whether to ask the nurse or risk trying to sneak in to see what she could find out when the door where Nick had disappeared opened, and he came out. He was as white as a sheet and there were tears on his cheeks. Maggie stood like a statue for a moment before she sped over. He didn't answer her query, looking right through her when she wrenched him around to face her. She shook him in her frustration and it was a measure of his state that he let her, as helpless as a rag doll in her hands. His chill struck through to her bones.

'Oh, Nick...' She was wearing flat shoes and had to reach to enfold him. His arms hung limply at his sides as she sought to warm and protect him with her body. She held him tightly, fearful he would slip away physically, as his mind seemed to have slipped away. Had they told him there was no hope? Was Laurie dead already, or had she suffered some horrendous mutilation? 'Nick, darling, please don't shut me out. Tell me... Tell me what's happened...'

He shuddered. His arms came up rigidly and she braced herself for rejection, but instead his hands gripped her waist so hard she almost cried out with the pain.

'The baby...' he said thickly. 'She lost the baby.'

'Oh, Nick...' Tears rushed to her eyes. 'Nick, I'm so
sorry...'

'My grandchild. My baby was going to be a mother
herself... My little Laurie...'

'How is she, Nick? How *is* Laurie?' Maggie asked ur-
gently, trying to penetrate his trance.

He shook his head. 'She...she's having a trans-
fusion. She lost a lot of blood. But they think she'll be
OK. She has a broken arm...some cuts from the wind-
screen but nothing serious...except the baby...there's
not going to be a baby. God, Maggie, she's so small and
white...and she knows... I can't reach her. God, how
she must hate me...she doesn't want me...she wants
the baby—she wants Cole—there's nothing I can give
her that she wants...'

His hands went around her, overlapping, anchoring
himself against her as his body began to shake. And she
held him, absorbing the powerful racking shudders,
gathering his tears in the curve of her throat where he
had buried his tormented face.

'You've given her your love, and your strength,'
Maggie whispered, turning him around the jut of the
corridor wall to give them a measure of privacy from
the rest of the waiting-room. 'She knows you love her
but it's only natural that she wants to see Finn, to share
her grief and loss with him. Because it's his loss, too.
They need each other now.'

'I'll kill him. If he's not already dead, I'll kill him,'
he ground out, but the words were lacking in force.

'No, you won't,' said Maggie confidently. 'You'll let
them mourn their baby together and offer them the con-
solation that there will be others...'

He stiffened, and she felt the coiling of his strength
and resistance but she refused to let him go. He dragged
his face across the soft, damp shoulder of her dress and
lifted his head. His face was haggard but he had never

looked more wonderful to her. Nick the strong had turned automatically into her arms in the moment of his greatest weakness.

'Still on his side, Maggie, even now?' he said bitterly.

'It's not a matter of sides, but of love. She loves you *both*, Nick; don't tear her apart by asking her to choose between you. They didn't deliberately set out to hurt you——'

'Or you?'

Maggie shook her head. 'There was never any danger of that. I'm not in love with *Finn*.'

He refused the gauntlet. 'Did *you* know about the baby?'

'Laurie told me last week.' He closed his eyes. 'Nick, she *couldn't* tell you——'

'No, I made that impossible,' he said tautly. 'By refusing to listen, to take her seriously as a woman.' He swallowed. 'I don't really know my daughter at all, do I?'

'You will. Just give her a chance. Give both of them a chance. You won't regret it.'

His hands dug into her back and he looked at her fully for the first time. 'She said that the elopement was all *her* doing,' he said wonderingly. 'Did you know that she actually *forged* my permission for the licence? She said that she didn't care whether the marriage was legal or not, she just wanted to be his wife...'

Maggie's eyes widened and Nick sucked in his breath. 'My God, you admire her for that,' he breathed. 'Yes, you would, wouldn't you, Maggie? You admire deviousness. And I thought *I* was being clever. You played us *all* for fools. Not just me—all of us!'

Maggie swallowed and tried to ease herself out of his hold, but the wounded tiger twitched his tail, his vitality returning.

'In view of what I've just learned I can't very well question Cole's manhood,' he said pleasantly, 'and in view of your delicious enthusiasm yesterday I *know* you're not frigid. So will you kindly enlighten me? How *did* you remain a virgin bride for five years? Or was the doctor who signed that startling document you left just another of your obliging lovers?'

She went crimson. She might have known that he'd find a way to doubt her! 'How dare you! You...you perverted pig! You woudln't know a virgin if...if...'

'If I were inside one?' he provided unblushingly. 'I'm no unicorn, Maggie. I'm just a man. And I've never made love to a virgin before. All I knew was that you were as sweet and hot and tight as I dreamed that you would be. I may have been stupidly unperceptive, but that appears to be par for the course. I thought my daughter was still a virgin, and look how mistaken I was about *that*...' He tailed off, and she knew he was thinking about the baby.

'There'll be other grandchildren for you, Nick...'

A ghost of amusement touched his hard mouth. 'I'm hoping there'll be other *children* for me. I'm not past the age of fatherhood yet, Maggie...'

'Yes, I noticed,' she gritted.

'Did that ruin another of your clever schemes?' He prodded the smouldering embers of her wounded heart. 'Were you hoping I'd forget contraception so that you could blackmail me with a pregnancy of your own?'

She struggled furiously with him, but this time *he* wasn't letting go. 'You're insanely paranoiac——'

'With good reason, wouldn't you say?' he said silkily, aware now of the way her mind was working. 'Are you angry at me, darling, for depriving you of your innocence without due ceremony? Whose fault was that? Who flaunted a string of supposed lovers in my face? And I suppose you're furious at me for wanting to take care of you. Did you *want* to fall pregnant the first time you ever made love? You silly little fool, you're not ready for motherhood yet.'

'Some expert you are, on who's ready for what!' she flung at him angrily.

'I know *I'm* not ready to father a child on you.' He ignored her outburst. 'Not until I've had some long-awaited answers to some very pertinent questions.' Maggie's mouth tightened mutinously and his eyes narrowed warningly on her lovely face. 'Don't test me, honey. I've jumped through hoops for you and now it's your turn.'

'Maggie?' A ragged groan provided a temporary reprieve. Finn was slumped against the wall behind them, fending off a plaintive white coat.

'Mr Cole, I told you we'd wheel you back——'

'Maggie, you said you'd find out about Laurie——'

Nick swung round, taking Maggie with him. He looked at the bloodied blond wraith and took a hissing breath. Finn didn't flinch under that implacable stare.

'She lost the baby,' Nick told him curtly.

Finn aged ten years in the space of a second. *'No!* Oh, no...*Laurie!* Where is she?' He tried to stumble past them but Nick caught a fistful of shirt and held him.

'We aren't married,' Finn blurted out in an agony of remorse. 'We were on our way back. We decided that it wasn't the way...it wasn't fair to any of us. We were going to confront you...tell you... Oh, God, I should never have let her talk me into it. I should have been strong——' His eyes were wretched with self-condemnation, and to her horror Maggie heard Nick callously twist the knife.

'Yes, you should have been. She needs that. Laurie is quiet but she's very strong-willed. She'll walk all over you if you let her, and despise you for it. If you don't assert yourself with her, she'll control you and not even realise that she's doing it...'

Finn stared at him blankly, not believing what he had just heard. It wasn't exactly approval, but it wasn't rejection either. It was parental advice. Nick turned his back on the stunned face that was rejuvenating before their eyes, not even bothering to watch Finn go.

'Now, where were we?'

'Thank you,' said Maggie huskily.

'For what? It was entirely selfish, I assure you,' Nick growled. 'I'm sick of your husband barging in on us.'

'Ex-husband.'

'Ah, yes—*that's* where we were. Your ill-starred marriage, your *first* marriage...'

The implications made her tremble, her mind scattering. 'You threw me out,' she blurted wildly. 'You never believe anything I say...'

'I believe you love me, and that's plenty to be going on with.'

'You threw me out in front of that horrible man,' she insisted weakly.

'That horrible man runs my household, but if he offends you I'll get rid of him. He's very good at his job, though, and he has a really rotten memory...'

'You made me feel like...like a whore——'

'With your natural talent in bed it was an easy mistake. It's certainly a career worth considering,' he agreed smoothly, jogging her out of her daze, restoring the fierce colour to her cheeks as she blazed at him in rage. He laughed and she hit him, and he laughed harder. People stared and Maggie felt dizzy with delight. She had pulled her clothes on any old how and not even stopped to brush her hair before she came out. She was a mess and this big, powerful man was making her feel wickedly desirable and desperately confused at the same time. He never said the expected thing...except when she didn't expect it!

'Nick——'

'Hush,' he gentled her. 'I love you. You hurt me. What was I supposed to do—smile, and let you grind me under your lovely heel? I'm not that kind of man and I never will be. So if you're looking for a gentle, complacent husband who'll give and never take you'd better say goodbye now.' Confidently, knowing she wouldn't; certain for the first time that she was totally his. 'And I need a wife who's not afraid of an occasional squall, who won't let me overpower her. You've never been afraid of me, have you, love?'

Maggie shook her head. 'You're a bully, but not a vicious bully,' she told him gravely. 'Besides, I know that brain beats brawn every time.'

His mouth twitched. 'We might fight, but I would never hurt you physically, Maggie.'

'I know. I...I'm sorry I lied to you, Nick, but I couldn't tell you...I didn't know you well enough and when I did, well, there were all sorts of complications. I...I didn't lie to you about *everything*...only when I couldn't help it.'

'Which was most of the time,' he offered pleasantly, so pleasantly that she quivered in his hands. 'Tell me now, Maggie, now that you have my whole and undivided and calm attention.'

Maggie opened her mouth and then snapped it shut as there came a loud burst of noise from the reception desk.

'Oh, no!' she groaned, leaning her head against Nick's chest to block out the sight of Paddy and Markham haranguing the nurse as Sam hovered ineffectually beside them.

'Ignore them, Maggie,' Nick told her, sensing the fragile moment slipping from his grasp.

'Oh, God, they're going to start a riot,' moaned Maggie as Markham inadvertently bumped a lank-haired youth boasting a gang patch. 'We've got to stop them——'

'Maggie——'

Paddy and Markham were now actually squaring up to each other, each claiming the right to be first in to see Finn. The nurse, quite rightly, favoured neither of them.

'They're going to hurt each other...and they still think Finn and I are married! Nick, you've got to do something. I know! Why don't we tell them that Finn has lost bits of his memory from the concussion and he doesn't remember that we were ever married. He only remembers me as a kind of sister. And then, in a few weeks or so, we could...what are you looking at me like that for?'

'My brain. It's finally defeated my stupid brawn! My God, Maggie, those two decrepit old goats over there! *They're* the reason for the whole fantastical farce, aren't they? You did this all for *them*...'

Once he had hit on the first premise it took little extra brainpower to ferret out the details. Nick was torn between fury, laughter and admiration.

'Maggie, you can't go on protecting them forever, even supposing they *want* to be protected! Look at them, they're in their element. Didn't I tell you that they *enjoy* their battles? Granted, five years ago they might have got a bit too reckless, but do you really think that they're going to jeopardise a lovely, comfortable feud for an empty victory at this late stage in their lives? Damn you, Maggie, there's such a thing as being *too* clever. You've been so busy playing your devious games you didn't notice the rules had changed. What you need now is a good impartial referee!'

He marched her, protesting furiously, over to where the two old men, true to form, were topping each other's insults of the Public Health System. Sam, meanwhile, was chatting up the attractive nurse for information, and making headway.

'Maggie! Where's Finn?' Paddy cried when he spied her. 'Why aren't you with him? Where's the doctor?'

'Doctor, hell! I called my specialist before I left home,' barked Markham, his moustache twitching with worry. 'Ah, Fortune, perhaps you know what's going on?'

'I surely do,' drawled Nick and, after setting their minds at rest about Finn, proceeded to tell them. Even in the form of edited highlights it made a fearful impact. For once in their lives Paddy and Markham were simultaneously speechless. Then, while they were still silently grappling with the past, Nick went on to tell them what the future had in store for them: in the short term a merger of their two companies, without furore or fuss, and a marriage—his and Maggie's. In the long term, after a suitably respectable engagement, a possible marriage for Finn and Laurie, with all children of both aforesaid marriages to receive shares in the merged company to be held in trust for their majority.

Even Maggie was impressed by his spur-of-the-moment ability to plug all conceivable loopholes.

'You mean... there was never any miscarriage!' Markham cried reproachfully to Maggie, when he had, with extreme reluctance, swallowed Nick's non-negotiable terms, subdued by the knowledge that it wasn't his old ex-partner who had been leading the ruthless raid on his shares.

'All these years,' Paddy wheezed dolefully. 'Five years waiting for a great-grandchild you never intended to have. You could have been having them by the dozen with someone else!'

'Oh, Paddy... Markham. .' Maggie sought for something to say that might help them over the shock.

'Maggie?'

She stared at an imperious, extended palm. 'Nick, we can't leave them——'

'I wasn't planning to. But I do think we need to find a storeroom around here somewhere.' She looked at him blankly, 'Or a broom cupboard... or an empty medical superintendent's office,' he explained, impatient with her obtuseness. 'Somewhere where we can be *private* for a few minutes, *alone...*' His eyes smouldered and she caught fire.

'Oh, yes...' She lowered her eyes demurely. 'Somewhere for you to humbly beg for my forgiveness and hand in marriage, you mean...'

His growling laugh promised her that, and much more, and she trotted meekly down the corridor after him. Suddenly she stopped and tugged her hand free, and went back.

Paddy and Markham regarded her with doleful expressions that held none of their former spark. They looked what they were: two old men approaching the end of full, rough-and-tumble lives.

'I just wanted you to know, that I love you both very much. I still consider myself to have *two* grandfathers.' Her brow wrinkled. 'I'd love to name my first son after one of you but, well, won't that offend the other? And I don't suppose it would be proper of me to ask *either* of you to vote his proxy, even if I could get Nick to approve...'

She heard the baying begin even before she and Nick had found their cosy linen cupboard.

'Troublemaker,' grinned Nick, trapping her against a convenient shelf. 'What am I going to do with you?'

Her eyes shone in the muted light of the naked bulb dangling above their heads. 'Love me...just love me.'

'Just?' He reached up and turned out the light and she gasped at his touch. 'Try and stop me...'

Of course she didn't.

And he did.

Harlequin ❖ _Presents_®

Coming Next Month

#1335 TOO STRONG TO DENY Emma Darcy
Elizabeth's principles lead her to ask Price Domenico, a top lawyer, to clear her of something she hasn't done. She needs his help no matter what it costs, though she hadn't reckoned on it costing her heart....

#1336 LOVE AT FIRST SIGHT Sandra Field
Bryden Moore is blind, but Casey Landrigan knows his real problem is his inability to love. Neither denies the growing attraction between them, but do they stand a chance when Bryden discovers Casey's true identity and the real reason she's vacationing next door?

#1337 WEB OF DESIRE Rachel Ford
The request to go to the Caribbean island of Halcyon Cay to restore valuable tapestries should have delighted Camilla. Instead it throws her into turmoil. For Halcyon Cay would have been _her_ island if it weren't for Matthew Corrigan.

#1338 BITTER SECRET Carol Gregor
The charismatic new owner of Sedbury Hall is an unwelcome intrusion into Sophie's well-controlled world. She's instantly attracted to him—but determined to live her life alone.

#1339 TIME FOR TRUST Penny Jordan
The traumas of Jessica's past mean she can no longer trust anyone—not even her parents. Then she falls in love with and weds Daniel Hayward—but would love, without trust, survive?

#1340 LET FATE DECIDE Annabel Murray
It's easy for Jenni to believe that meeting Clay Cunningham's blue eyes across a crowded marketplace was meant to happen. But it's not so easy for Jenni to cope with her feelings once Clay makes it clear that any relationship between the two will be on his terms.

#1341 THE DEVIL'S EDEN Elizabeth Power
Coralie Rhodes—working under the name Lee Roman—desperately needs an interview with Jordan Colyer's famous uncle, to rescue her flagging magazine But events of eight years ago had convinced Jordan that Coralie is a gold digger Will he take his revenge now?

#1342 CONDITIONAL SURRENDER Wendy Prentice
Kate is shocked when Greg Courtney, her boss, reveals he's been burning with desire for her since their first meeting. Kate finds him attractive,too, but Greg is a cynic who doesn't believe in love. Kate is a romantic and knows that it's essential.

Available in February wherever paperback books are sold, or through Harlequin Reader Service:

In the U.S.
901 Fuhrmann Blvd.
P O Box 1397
Buffalo, N.Y 14240-1397

In Canada
P O Box 603
Fort Erie, Ontario
L2A 5X3

REBECCA YORK

Labeled a "true master of intrigue" by *Rave Reviews*, best-selling author Rebecca York makes her Harlequin Intrigue debut with an exciting suspenseful new series.

It looks like a charming old building near the renovated Baltimore waterfront, but inside 43 Light Street lurks danger . . . and romance.

Let Rebecca York introduce you to:

> *Abby Franklin*—a psychologist who risks everything to save a tough adventurer determined to find the truth about his sister's death. . . .
>
> *Jo O'Malley*—a private detective who finds herself matching wits with a serial killer who makes her his next target. . . .
>
> *Laura Roswell*—a lawyer whose inherited share in a development deal lands her in the middle of a murder. And she's the chief suspect. . . .

These are just a few of the occupants of 43 Light Street you'll meet in Harlequin Intrigue's new ongoing series. Don't miss any of the 43 LIGHT STREET books, beginning with #143 LIFE LINE.

And watch for future LIGHT STREET titles, including #155 SHATTERED VOWS (February 1991) and #167 WHISPERS IN THE NIGHT (August 1991).